A Scottish Wedding

A Scottish Wedding

HILARIA ALEXANDER

A Scottish Wedding
Copyright © 2017 Hilaria Alexander

All rights reserved. No part of this book may be reproduced or transmitted in any form or by any means, electronic or mechanical, including photocopying, recording, or by any information storage and retrieval system without the written permission of the author, except for the use of brief quotations in a review.

This is a work of fiction. Names, characters, businesses, places, events and incidents are either the products of the author's imagination or used in a fictitious manner. Any resemblance to actual persons, living or dead, or actual events is purely coincidental.

This book is licensed for your personal enjoyment only. This book may not be re-sold or given away to other people. If you are reading this book and did not purchase it, or it was not purchased for your use only, then you should return it to the seller and purchase your own copy. Thank you for respecting the author's work.

Published: Hilaria Alexander 2017
hilaria_alexander@outlook.com
Editing: Editing by C. Marie
Proofreading: Proofing Style
Cover Design: Samantha Leigh Design
Photo: Adobe Stock
Formatting: AB Formatting

Chapter 1

SAM

When I was a little girl, I didn't much care for fairy tales.

Don't get me wrong, I loved movies, but more than being concerned with romance and falling for Prince Charming, I was interested in the setting.

Where did these people live? How could I go there?

I didn't understand that the actors were people who acted in a studio.

I didn't understand that when my father said, "I worked on that movie," it meant he was on set with the actors. I thought they'd given him a special pass to reach a faraway land where he filmed the lives of the characters.

I thought the stories *and* the places in the movies were real, and what I wanted the most was to be in a fantasy land like the one in *Labyrinth*, or even the scarier dark kingdom

A Scottish Wedding

of *Return to Oz*. I thought the kids of *The Goonies* lived in an alternate reality similar to my own, and I wanted to be able to go on a treasure hunt alongside them.

Bananas, I know.

It was only later, when I reached puberty, that I fell for the unlikely fairy tales romantic comedies tried to sell.

It wasn't about the movie anymore; it was all about the swoon and the romance.

It was all about the bad boy with a heart of gold and the easygoing smile.

When I became a teen, I started getting *hungry* for that kind of love you only see in movies. Even though I now understood it was all pretend, I still wanted to trade places with Julia Stiles and be the subject of Heath Ledger's affection in *10 Things I Hate About You*. I wanted to be Drew Barrymore, getting kissed for the first time by Michael Vartan in the middle of a baseball field in *Never Been Kissed*.

A few years later, I came to the conclusion that as much as I loved romantic comedies, they were the sum of all the lies women tell themselves.

First, my parents decided to split, which severely tarnished my belief in "happily ever after." Then, I realized that guys are a galaxy far, far away from how they are portrayed in movies and books—well, at least most of them.

Even when I thought I'd finally found the one, I was faced with a harsh reality.

Loving, handsome, faithful boyfriends were the stuff of dreams.

At least that's what I thought, until *him*.

Before Hugh MacLeod came into my life, I'd been ready to throw in the towel.

I was done giving my heart to lying, cheating sons of a bitch.

Hugh restored my faith in love, and had just asked me to share the adventure of a lifetime with *him*.

God, I love this man.

He kissed me on the lips, softly, and my head started spinning.

Is this really happening?

"We're getting married?" It came out as a question, although I knew I wasn't dreaming. I was awake, the ring on my finger was real, and the man in front of me was even better. He had already given me his heart, and now he wanted to live the rest of our lives together.

He nodded, a tight-lipped smile stretching on his face.

My eyes danced between him and the ring, my chest crushed by a juggernaut of emotions, my head swimming in a sea of serotonin.

The cottage, the proposal, the emotion in his eyes—it was all too much. I felt like I needed a minute. I needed to sit down, but there wasn't any furniture in the house, and I needed him for a minute, too—a minute, an hour, an entire night. Oh, how I'd missed him.

I raised myself up on my tiptoes and kissed him, running my fingers through his curls. He smelled divine, a mix of mint and musk. His jaw, freshly shaved, was just so delectable. I had to cover it with kisses; it just *had* to be done.

He was mine, and I was going to show him for the rest of my days how much I loved him. Suddenly, my mind went to a few months back, when I thought I'd lost him forever.

My chest tightened, and an uncomfortable knot grew in my throat.

Ah, dammit. That did it.

The tears I had managed to tuck away just a few minutes ago spilled onto my cheeks, and a few seconds later, they transformed into full-on crying. Through blurry eyes, I could see my fiancé looking at me with the utmost confusion.

"Sam, what's wrong?"

"Y-You . . . I-I . . ." I babbled, unable to form any comprehensible words between sobs. He frowned, narrowing his eyes at my ridiculous reaction. I was gripping his sweater, as if he was about to slip out of my hold. He held me tighter to him, and my palms pressed on his chest. I could hear his heart beating as fast as mine and I breathed in, trying to calm my stupid, stupid self. Hopefully in a minute I'd be able to explain, and maybe he wouldn't want to reconsider and take back his marriage proposal.

"*Mo chridhe*," he said softly, using the Scottish words that meant *my heart*. "What is it? You were smiling just a moment ago." A low chuckle escaped his lips and he kissed the top of my head. I inhaled deeply and then let out a breath, trying to calm myself down, telling myself everything was okay.

This is ridiculous. I had some explaining to do.

I wiped the runny makeup from under my eyes and sniffled. I straightened myself up, pressed my hands on his chest once more, and looked up into his wary eyes.

"I'm sorry. I don't want you to worry. It's stupid." I pursed my lips together, taking in one more deep breath. "I am happy—*so* happy." I smiled at him and he seemed to believe it, but I knew I wasn't making much sense. "I just . . . I suddenly thought of when I had to leave at the beginning of this year . . ." I lowered my eyes and frowned, remembering how hard it'd been to leave him.

His chest rose under my hands as he inhaled deeply. I knew it was something he didn't like to talk about. He wasn't happy with me when I was let go and decided to leave, but I had seen no other choice at the time. I had to do what was best for him, even if it broke my heart. I looked up to him and noticed his eyes were the color of the Scotland sky on one of those rare, good sunny days—the same type that had welcomed me back today—but they were heavy with worry.

I cleared my throat. "When I left Scotland at the beginning of this year, I thought I might have lost you forever. The way we said goodbye . . . I didn't know if you'd ever want to talk to me again. I didn't know if you could ever forgive me."

"You have nothing to apologize for. I shouldn't have left things like that." The tone of his voice was firm but reassuring. I knew he didn't need any explanation, but we'd never talked about it, and I needed him to know. I had to tell him how elated I felt.

"Until that night at the Oscars, I often thought there was a possibility you hated me. I didn't know if you really understood why I *had* to leave after I got fired. I couldn't stop thinking about the look in your eyes when you left."

He tipped my chin up with a finger and covered my lips with his. He gave me a peck, and then another one. "What are you trying to say, Sam? Are you wondering if I really understood that you left to protect my career? That you decided to leave so I wouldn't have more problems with the network? No, at first I didn't understand it. I was . . . blinded by rage, and I couldn't bear the thought of losing ye." He pressed his lips in a hard line, his jaw taut, eyes clouded by the bitter memories of our goodbye, one of the roadblocks that had been in our way since we'd started falling for each other. "I admit, I was mad at you, Sam—really mad. I thought you were giving up on us."

I closed my eyes and shook my head. A lonely tear escaped my eye and I sniffled again.

"I wasn't. God, of course I wasn't."

"I know that . . . *now*." His lips curved to the side into that honest, charming smile that made my heart flutter. "It took a whole day of drinking and feeling miserable. I woke up wasted on the floor of my trailer and I was there for hours, immersed in your scent. I don't know how long I stared at the ceiling before I finally figured out you left . . . *for me*."

"I couldn't bear the thought of you thinking I didn't love you enough to fight for you. The way we left things . . . it broke my heart. I was just trying to make the best of it, I suppose."

"You were trying to do what was best for me. I ken that now, Sam."

"Your dreams are important to me. I thought I was doing the right thing." He nodded and smiled silently, his eyes alive with a kindling spark. "I will always try to do what's best for you, and from now on, I will always try to do what's best for *us*." My eyes fell on my beautiful ring, part of me still incredulous that the man in front of me wanted to share his world with me for the rest of our lives. He kissed me, circling his tongue with mine, deep and maddeningly slow, awakening other parts of me that had been missing him for too long. Desire made romance scoot to the passenger seat and took the lead. I needed him.

"I need to have you, *right now*. It's been too long," I mumbled, my mind rendered incapacitated by his kisses. It was amazing the way his lips and his tongue could make me completely incoherent and crazed for more. "Take off your clothes, MacLeod," I told him, my voice low and raspy.

His eyes twinkled as his lips curved into a playful grin.

"But there's no furniture in this house," he teased.

"Like I care. Take off your clothes—now," I commanded, tugging at his blue sweater. The look on his face was equal parts cocky and amused, but it just left me frustrated and wondering why the hell wasn't he naked already.

"Come with me," he said, and his eyes brimmed with excitement and mischief.

He led me to a closet in the corner of the master bedroom. We'd gotten sidetracked, and I hadn't even seen what he'd done with the rest of the upstairs level—not that there was that much left to see. It was a small cottage, after all. He led me inside and turned on the light. I peeked in and noticed a few things wrapped in heavy-duty plastic. He pulled a large rolled-up mattress out of the closet.

"Help me out, Sam."

I took the opposite end of the bundle and lifted it up as best I could. The damn thing was heavy.

"Where do you want this?" I asked

"By the windows, where we were standing."

A Scottish Wedding

We dropped it down to the floor.

"What now?"

"Now we try to open this," Hugh said as he tried to tear the thick plastic, but he couldn't get through it with his fingers. I looked at him in horror as he grabbed a corner of the material and tried to break it with his teeth.

"Stop! Are you insane? What if you break your teeth? You think Abarath could charm all those chicks with a crooked smile?" I said, hiding my teeth behind my lips, making a face.

He responded with an eye roll and a shrug, and I laughed. "You're ridiculous. Move," I said as I pulled a pocketknife out of my jacket.

"A pocketknife? Where did you get that?"

"My dad gave it to me. He said an adventurous woman like myself shouldn't go anywhere without one," I said, straightening up.

A small laugh escaped his lips and he shook his head.

"And why did you think you needed that today?"

I shrugged. "I decided to bring it along in case I was wrong about your whereabouts and got lost in the middle of the glen."

I tore through the plastic with the small, pointy knife, and Hugh broke through the rest of it. The foam mattress slowly unrolled and opened up on the floor. We took the plastic off and threw it in a corner of the room then tried to smooth the corners of the mattress. I was reading the instructions when I was unceremoniously thrown down on it.

"Hey! It says here you're supposed to 'let the mattress breathe' and 'take shape' for two or three days . . . I'm not sure this is a good idea."

"Two or three days?" he asked with a scoff. "I can't wait that long," he added with a smirk. He took off his sweater, revealing his broad, strong chest in all its glory. I didn't know which was hotter: him or the look of determination he got in his eyes right before we made love. It was the sexiest thing ever. I kicked off my shoes and took off my socks as he knelt on the mattress next to me.

He unbuckled his belt and pulled down his jeans as I semi-frantically removed my clothing. We kept stealing glances, as if it was the first time we'd seen each other naked. Like I said, it had been a while.

"Bollocks! I forgot something," he muttered as he walked to another corner of the room where a door hid what looked like a linen closet. He grabbed a blanket, one with colors I had seen before. It was the MacLeods of Harris tartan.

I smiled.

Once upon a time, two MacLeod clans existed, or so I had been told: the MacLeods of Lewis and the MacLeods of Harris. The MacLeods of Lewis' tartan was the one with the yellow and black colors, and their motto was "Shine, not burn." History said the MacLeods of Lewis clan was wiped out by the Mackenzies—I'd learned that from Hugh's father and his brother Tamhas a few months back. Hugh's father was a Celtic languages professor at Oxford, and Tamhas was a teacher who had majored in history while attending the University of Edinburgh.

While the tartan of the MacLeods of Lewis was yellow and black, the one of the MacLeods of Harris was blue and green, with thin yellow and red stripes. I wondered how tartan patterns had been picked once upon a time, who decided what colors they would be. That was a question for Hugh's father, no doubt. Although a professor of Celtic languages, my future father-in-law was also an expert in all things Scottish.

Hugh knelt back on the bare mattress, opened the blanket with his family's colors, and covered my semi-naked body with it. His eyes didn't leave mine as he took off the rest of his clothes. I skimmed out of my jeans under the plaid and lifted it for him to lie next to me.

We were finally naked, skin to skin, after being apart for weeks. Forget about "Shine, not burn"—I was *burning* with anticipation. I needed him to take me, right that minute, but I didn't want to fast-forward through a single moment. It was too beautiful to miss. He embraced me and held me tight to him as his mouth placed small, chaste kisses along my forehead.

"Do you remember what my clan motto says?" he asked with a grin.

"Hold fast," I replied with a delighted smile. I remembered it well, because Hugh's father had told me the story behind it when I stayed with them at Christmas.

Supposedly, the motto was born when the chief of the clan wrestled a bull to the ground and the crowd cheered for him to "hold fast."

In a way, as soon as I'd heard it, I thought it fit Hugh MacLeod perfectly.

Only, in my head, I thought of him as the bull that had crashed into my life and turned it upside down—for the better, obviously. I laughed softly as Hugh's piercing blue eyes skimmed over my body.

He was the bull, all right, and I was his target.

"That's right, Sam. Hold fast," he said with a grin. "We're in it for the long run."

Chapter 2

SAM

I was never too fond of the feeling of wool on my skin. Most times, it made my skin feel prickly, and living in Los Angeles, I wasn't used to heavy fabrics.

However, there was nothing like being wrapped in the tartan that belonged to the man you loved. The wool had a certain softness to it, and it felt warm and . . . durable. It reminded me of older times, when things were passed down from family member to family member, just like the ring on my finger.

I couldn't help staring at it, even now that my husband-to-be was on top of me. The sparkle of the diamonds distracted me, and yet, it also reminded me of how deep and pure the love my man had for me was. I wanted all of it.

"I want all of you," I whispered, kissing his lips as he leaned down.

"You have me," he replied.

His erection pressed against my hip, and I opened my legs to accommodate him. I grabbed his smooth, hard cock with my hand and pressed it against my entrance. He slid in, filling me and stretching me. The ache I had felt for weeks could finally be satisfied, and since I'd decided to go on birth control a few months ago, now we didn't even need to worry about protection. It could just be me and him, skin to skin.

I loved seeing him get lost inside of me. It was the biggest turn-on.

"You are so beautiful, Sam."

His words, mixed with the fresh memories of his proposal, made me tear up again.

"I love you," I told him, trying my best to hold back the tears.

"You know I will never stop loving you," he said, thrusting into me deeper. "It's me and you from now on, *neach gaoil*."

HUGH

I let her sleep a bit, figuring she must be exhausted after her flight and the trek all the way up to St. Martin. I reckoned the proposal was probably quite the shock, even though a good one. She was sleeping on her right side, and I took a picture of her with her left hand stretched on top of the MacLeod tartan.

A Scottish Wedding

I would have married her the next day, or even that night if I could have.

Being apart from her had been the worst thing I'd ever had to endure. It lasted barely two months, and it was just enough time to be certain of the fact that I didn't want to spend one more day without her.

My phone buzzed, and I took it out of my pocket to see who it was.

So? How did it go? Can I call her yet? Hugh, I'm dying here!

Cecilia, always *so* dramatic. Of course, when Sam had told her which day she'd be arriving, Cecilia wanted to organize a little get-together. That was before I'd informed her I had big plans for us, so I had to let her in on the whole thing, and ever since, I had been afraid she would let something slip.

"Please, Hugh, I know how to keep a secret. Don't you trust me?" she'd told me in a semi-offended tone.

Honestly? I didn't, not a hundred percent. Cecilia was . . . well, Cecilia. She was a good friend, generous, and enthusiastic, but she could talk a lot. I'd told her I wouldn't forgive her if she'd accidentally ruined the surprise.

SAM

It was dark when I woke up. I wrapped the tartan around my shoulders, covering my naked body, and went looking for him.

He was downstairs, and he'd lit a fire. He was sitting on the floor, right in front of it. My eyes scanned the place once more. I couldn't believe this was the same rundown place we'd come to last year. It was so much prettier, and although small, all the updates made it look incredibly functional. I laughed to myself, thinking we'd better get some furniture soon if we didn't want to keep sitting on our asses.

"Sorry I fell asleep," I told him as I joined him by the fire.

A slow, lazy grin spread across his face.

"You were out cold." His eyes took me in, naked and wrapped in the MacLeod tartan, and became clouded with lust. I smiled to myself. He leaned in for a soft peck and I leaned against his shoulder, staring at the fire, fighting against my heavy eyelids.

A yawn escaped my lips, and Hugh gave me a concerned look.

"I'll be okay. Just need some time to wake up."

"Do you think you're up for a bit of celebrating?"

I smiled at his accent making a more marked appearance. "What do you have in mind?"

"Well, there's actually some place we need to be. You better go get dressed, love."

A Scottish Wedding

She crossed the pub with the fury of a woman on a mission, and *I* was her objective. She came straight for me, wrapping me in a bear hug despite her petite frame before I could even say a word.

When she finally let me go, I could barely mutter, "I am so happy to see you!" before she started assaulting Hugh with questions.

"About time! I mean, were you going to keep her hostage, mate?" Cecilia asked in a brash tone. I wasn't sure if I should laugh at her for being so eager to see me or get mad at her for being so mean to my fiancé.

Hugh was standing behind me and scoffed at Cecilia's accusations.

After I'd left, Cecilia had become his makeup artist, and they had gotten much closer. It wasn't really that surprising. My ex-flatmate had what I'd call a *hurricane personality*. She was the kind of person who was going to drop into your life with the magnitude of a natural disaster. Fortunately, she wasn't mean or vindictive; she was just energetic and stubborn, and that alone was sometimes too much to deal with. But, she meant well, and she was a loyal friend. She'd always taken my side and rooted for Hugh and me when we had to keep our relationship secret.

She also stood by my side when the network let me go. She even sent me messages—although I hadn't asked her to—keeping tabs on my man at a time when he wasn't technically mine.

The two months spent apart were some of the bleakest days of my entire life. I knew leaving had been the right choice, even though it hadn't been the easiest. I'd taken the job in Scotland on a whim, to escape Los Angeles and the drama I was partly responsible for. When things between Hugh and me got serious, it became evident that the network's executives were not above playing petty games, and I knew I had to make a choice.

In the end, I *had* to go so Hugh would have his chance to shine and could give *Abarath* one hundred percent.

"Cecilia, stop," I told her with a small laugh. "I fell asleep."

She suddenly stopped glaring at Hugh, and she looked me in the eye.

"Bollocks," she said slowly, enunciating every syllable. "You don't have to defend him all the time, Sam."

"I'm not!" I tried to argue but ended up laughing, shaking my head in disbelief. I leaned in and took her face in my hands then kissed her on both cheeks, as Europeans did.

She looked instantly mollified by my gesture.

"I'm happy to see you too, you know," I told her in a sweet tone, trying to get back in her good graces—and it worked. A smile spread across her face and she latched her arms around my neck, hugging me again.

"Oh goodness, Sam, I am *so happy* to see you!" Her voice came out in a shriek, and I squeezed my eyes shut as she shouted in my ear. It didn't matter, though, because I was just as happy to be reunited with my friend.

"Come," she said, grabbing my hand and pulling me along. I turned around to smile at Hugh, who followed closely and smiled patiently at the drama queen.

As it turned out, every one of our closest friends from last year's crew had been at the pub for the last two hours . . . waiting on us. Hugh had told them to meet up at Munro's

A Scottish Wedding

at a certain time, but no one except Oliver and Cecilia knew what he'd been planning.

I spent the next hour working the room and catching up with the people I'd had to reluctantly leave behind at the beginning of the year. Everyone was pleasantly shocked to see my engagement ring, and I felt my face grow warmer with each celebratory round of whisky and every *slainte*. In fact, I was getting noticeably tipsy.

One face was missing: Jake, the set decorator I had sometimes flirted with before Hugh and I got hot and heavy. Jake had been a real troubadour on the set of season one, collecting numerous hookups during the months in St. Martin.

Thankfully, I had been smart enough to never get involved with him. I'd been burned badly by my breakup with Eric, and Jake reminded me too much of him.

Jake had been hired to work on the set of *Game of Thrones*, so he wouldn't be back this season. He was happy to be working on an even bigger production, and women on that set didn't play hard to get, according to him. *Ewww*. I'd heard this specific piece of news from Cecilia, but I knew about his job because we kept in touch from time to time via text messages. They were always innocent and very sporadic and yet, that was all it took to make Hugh a *wee bit* jealous. I snickered at the thought of Hugh being jealous of Jake, because there was no competition whatsoever.

Jake was handsome and sexy, but fickle like a candle.

Hugh MacLeod was . . . the whole package, and he was *mine*. Still, I couldn't be too upset by the fact that Hugh was jealous of Jake. In fact, it had been the jealousy he harbored toward my coworker that had caused him to act on his feelings for me; jealousy was the spark that ignited Hugh MacLeod's lust, and eventually his love. He had seen us flirt one night at the pub—during my *superb* rendition of Ginuwine's "Pony"—and his testosterone-fueled envy produced such a tizzy that he *had* to have me.

I looked up at him, holding my bottom lip between my teeth.

"What is it?" he asked.

"Nothing," I replied with a smile and a shake of my head.

"You're thinking about something . . . and you think you can't tell me?" he asked with a frown.

I hesitated. "I was wondering . . . are you sure you had nothing to do with Jake getting a job with *Game of Thrones* and not coming back for season two?"

The broad smile that stretched on his face was blinding and infectious. Was he not going to hide it at all? He wasn't even going to try?

"Trust me," he said, "I had nothing to do with it. If I had, I'd take credit for it. That . . . what did you call him before?"

"Sleazeball."

"That *sleazeball* has no place on this set." He laughed, and I joined him. Jake wasn't a bad guy, but no one could deny it—he was a sleazeball. He was a shameless flirt who would always kiss and tell.

As the night progressed and I saw old and new friends—new crewmembers who'd be working on season two—I learned that Jake had been replaced by a beautiful and busty blonde by the name of Gretchen.

We exchanged a few words and she seemed like a nice

girl, but as soon as she was out of earshot, Cecilia made a face and some comment about the girl looking like a bimbo.

"Come on, Cece. You don't need to go full-on mean girl now, do you? I bet Oliver is not even going to look at her."

"Oh, it's not Oliver I'm worried about, but I would watch her around Hugh, if you know what I mean," she said in a low tone, raising her eyebrows and turning her head in the direction of Gretchen, who was now chatting up some actors, including Hugh.

"Why would you say something like that? I-I . . . I just got engaged," I replied, almost speechless.

"You're welcome," she said in a serious tone. I narrowed my eyes at her and she burst into a laugh and bumped her shoulder against my arm. "I'm kidding, you *gullible* American!" She walked away toward the bar, glass in hand, probably looking for a refill.

"You're so going to pay for this, Cecilia!" I grumbled before she got too far away.

She was *joking*, but what a stupid thing to say.

I'd never been too jealous when it came to Hugh, because he never gave me any reason to be concerned, but sometimes I couldn't help but worry, especially after what had happened with Eric.

My last relationship had gone up in smoke right in front of my eyes when my boss and my boyfriend took their work liaison to a whole new level. Sometimes I wondered how much longer they would have been sneaking around my back if I hadn't seen them kissing at the Golden Globes and if I hadn't told the entire world about their affair.

Cecilia was right about one thing: I was gullible. I had been in the past, that was for sure. Maybe it wouldn't hurt to try to keep a vigilant eye, just as a safety measure.

I mindlessly joined Cecilia and turned around with my back against the wooden bar, facing our group of friends.

"Seriously, you are a prankster's dream," she said with a smug smile, twisting a thin cocktail straw into her drink.

"I would stop it right now if I were you," I replied in a low growl, matching the tone of my voice with the unamused expression on my face.

"I know, I know. That was a cruel joke, but . . . come on! The man just gave you a house and put a ring on your finger."

"It was a tasteless joke."

She lowered her eyes and raised her shoulder in a shrug just as a smile stretched across her face. "You're right, I'm sorry. It's just that . . . it's too much fun to see you getting all worked up, Sam. I missed you. I missed *this*."

Cecilia going soft on me? *Impossible.* I narrowed my eyes at her and she nodded, swearing it was the truth.

"I really missed you, Sam, and as excited as I am to be with Oliver, I'm going to miss living with you. Things are great, but it's different than from last year, you know?"

"Awwww, Cece." I tilted my head in her direction and gave her a knowing look. "I missed you, too." I reached for her hand and squeezed it, and she squeezed it back. With her other hand, she took a swig of her cocktail and nodded thoughtfully, placing her glass down on the bar.

"Plus, I am not going to have anyone cooking for me anymore. Oliver is shit at it!"

I hastily let go of her hand and groaned.

"So that's the real reason why you miss me! You're such a slag!"

A Scottish Wedding

She laughed impenitently, not a hint of shame on her face. A moment later, I was distracted by another beautiful, rich laugh coming from across the pub.

Gretchen.

I glanced at the bosomy, bubbly blonde impressing the circle of men around her—most of the male cast, in fact. Gretchen had her hand all over Mika's arm—he played Kjell, Abarath's best friend and second in command. I had only read three books of the series and some of Kjell's past hadn't been revealed yet, but from what I knew so far, he had come from a Scandinavian kingdom, was a skilled swordsman, and was a healer. He wasn't your average type of "healer" either—his hands had healing power, but that was a skill his character kept under wraps. Only Abarath and a few others knew about it.

Gretchen was telling Mika something, leaning in, and they were laughing together as the rest of the guys watched and laughed, all too eager to get in on the action and have a bit of Gretchen's attention.

Hugh was laughing as well, although he seemed a bit distant and removed from the general conversation. He raised his glass to his lips, and that's when his eyes met mine. I saw the smile in his eyes before I could see the one on his lips. He swallowed his drink and lowered the glass, and then raised it in the air, nodding in my direction.

Butterflies fluttered in my stomach as I replied to his toast with a shy smile.

Jokes and scumbag ex-boyfriends aside, I knew I had nothing to worry about.

That man is mine.

Just the thought of him sparked another wave of

desire. Warmth spread in my lower belly, and suddenly, I had an idea.

Last year we had to keep things under wraps and could never be seen in public, let alone do something a bit more . . . *risky*.

Bathroom sex had never sounded as enticing as it did right then, especially with the bedroom eyes he was giving me from across the room.

"We should sing a song," Cecilia said, interrupting my daydream.

"It's not karaoke night," I replied without taking my eyes off Hugh.

"I'm sure they'll make an exception for *us*."

I turned in her direction. "Go ahead, the floor is yours."

"We should do it together. The *only* time we sang together, you got whisked away. We should celebrate," she insisted.

"Another night, maybe. I'm a bit worn out from my flight. Besides, I have a different kind of celebrating in mind." I couldn't stop the smile on my face from growing wider. Hugh, on the other side of the pub, still had his eyes locked on me. Cecilia turned around and finally caught up on what was going on.

"Oh, I see. You're hopeless, Sam." She let out a small laugh and I shook my head, disagreeing with her.

"I'm not hopeless, I'm helpless. I just can't help myself," I told her before walking away, my eyes fixed on my man.

"Fine, don't sing with me. I'll make sure to dedicate Selena's 'Hands to Myself' to you as soon as you two make it out of that bathroom."

"Sounds good to me," I replied with a wink, taking her up on her challenge.

"You're so bad," he whispered.

"Shush, you love it," I replied as I locked the stall door behind us.

"I do." His accent was deeper whenever he said that, and I couldn't help but fantasize about the day he was going to say that in response to taking me as his wife.

For the time being, he was taking me elsewhere.

"Bad girl," he whispered in my ear, his erection pressing against my back. I turned around and he was grinning, his eyes wild with desire. He pinned me against the wall, one of his hands grabbing a fistful of my hair.

His mouth captured mine and his tongue traced the shape of my lips before wrapping around my tongue in a fluid tempo. He broke the kiss too soon and my back arched, my hips looking for more friction. One of his hands slid under my shirt, pulling my bra down, teasing my heavy breast and my hard nipple.

"What if someone finds us here?"

"Unlikely," I replied in a whisper as his mouth placed slow, deep, searing kisses on my neck.

"Why do you say that?"

"Because . . . I just sent several trays of food to the tables. No one is coming in here unless their bladder is ready to burst."

"So clever," he teased. "But what if they do? What if someone comes in here?"

"Well, in that case . . . I bet you can be *very* still . . . and very quiet, too. Can't you?"

He hummed, but his eyebrows were pressed together.

"What is it? Don't tell me you've never had bathroom sex before."

A grin flashed across his face and he shrugged. "What if I haven't?"

He kissed my lips again and parted them with his tongue, but this time I broke the kiss.

"Wait . . . you've never had sex in a public restroom?" I asked, locking eyes with him.

He replied with a small shrug and a tight-lipped Mona Lisa smile.

"I'm deflowering you?" I couldn't hide the hint of shock in my tone or the smile on my face.

"What can I say? The situation never presented itself," he said softly, fiddling with a lock of my long black hair.

"Nu-uh, I find that hard to believe."

He traced the tip of his nose along my jaw, the sensation sending a jolt of electricity down my spine. I grabbed his *arse* and pressed him against me. One of my hands traveled to the front of his pants, stroking his erection over the denim.

He let out a low growl as he started placing kisses on my neck again, down to my collarbone.

"Believe it, my beautiful . . . dangerous . . . incredibly sexy fiancée." Each pause was a deep kiss on my skin. He knelt in front of me and lifted my shirt, kissing my stomach. He unbuttoned my pants and hastily pulled them down to my ankles along with my underwear in a move that was so sudden, it almost made me flinch. He kissed my belly, down to the little path of hair. He parted my lips with a finger and flicked his tongue along my most sensitive spot, making my knees buckle. He looked up and grinned at me, delighted by my reaction. He unlaced one of my boots and took it off then pulled off my pants, and my underwear with them.

He looked up at me, a wicked grin stretched across his face.

"Phase one completed."

"Phase one?" I asked, confused.

"The undressing. I now have access to you."

"Oh."

"Yeah, 'oh.' You better be wearing a skirt next time we do this." *Next time?* His eyes were full of mischief, and he looked so delicious I licked my lips.

"Yes sir," I replied in a low, submissive tone as I unbuttoned his pants. He pulled them down, freeing his erection of both jeans and boxer briefs.

"Phase two is now complete."

"You're such a nerd," I teased.

"Am I?" He stared at me, turning the smolder all the way up. *What a tease.* "Let's see what you think of this nerd in a few minutes."

A small laugh escaped my lips as his gaze set my skin on fire. I couldn't think when he looked at me that way.

"What's phase three?" I mumbled incoherently when I found my voice.

He tilted his head to the side, the corner of his lips curled up. His eyes twinkled as the words came out of his beautiful pink lips.

"Phase three, coming up."

He squatted just barely and grabbed my legs on each side, lifting them up and wrapping them around his waist. I locked my hands around his neck and kissed him, slow and deep. I was aware of only three things in that moment: the cold bathroom tiles pressed against my ass, his warm cock teasing my entrance, and how turned on I was by this man.

My man. My love.

"Phase three: contact."

"Such a nerd," I whispered in his ear, biting his earlobe gently.

"Nerd, aye?" he teased, filling me with one thrust. I gasped.

"Yes," I teased, but my voice was already breathy and heavy with need.

He adjusted his hands on my ass, pressing harder into me, settling into a rhythm that was bound to bring me to the edge soon—very soon.

In fact, I was already seeing white lights flashing in front of my eyes.

By the way he kept moving and thrusting into me, I wasn't going to last long.

And by the way he grunted, I guessed he wasn't either.

"Fuck, Sam, you're so damn sexy. How am I supposed to resist you?"

"You don't have to. That's the beauty of it." The words came out in a strangled, high-pitched voice as I surrendered to the feeling of ecstasy taking over my body.

His release followed soon after, echoing my grunts and low moans that sent a wave of oxytocin rushing through my body. I could never get tired of listening to him come

A Scottish Wedding

undone inside me.

The bathroom door opened just as he put me down, and a woman's voice filled the space with laughter. I scrambled to pick up my jeans, and we stared at each other tight-lipped and wide-eyed as we listened to the woman talking. She was on the phone, talking to a friend. I tried to figure out if she was part of our group, but I couldn't place her voice.

"You'll never bloody guess! I'm in St. Martin to visit my parents, and guess what? The entire cast of *Abarath* is here. I overheard they're going to start shooting in a couple weeks. We totally need to come up and stalk the cast. Have you seen the arse on that Hugh MacLeod? He makes me want to flick the bean any time he's naked on that show!"

I was already pursing my lips together at the mention of Hugh's *arse*, but I frowned because "flick the bean" wasn't something I was familiar with. When Hugh pointed at my vagina, I almost let out a laugh, but thankfully he covered my mouth with his hand, giving me a reprimanding look. He brought a finger to his mouth and told me to be quiet.

"I know! And I haven't told you the best part! I think I heard someone say he's here, or *was* here at the pub. I know, I know, I need to find him. I wonder if he's still with that American floozie."

My eyebrows shot up at her words, and Hugh brought his finger up to his mouth again. I was mostly amused, really. It was the first time someone had ever referred to me as an *American floozie*.

"Wish me luck and maybe I'll meet that tight, fine ass. Bye, love!"

By the jingle of her bracelets, I guessed she was washing and drying her hands. Her heels clicked on the floor and she walked out of the bathroom, slamming the door behind her. As soon as I heard the click of the door, I leaned into his chest and started laughing. It was only seconds later that his body started shaking with laughter as well, the sound of it muffled as he pressed his mouth against my hair. We held each other for a few more seconds, and then I gave his ass a squeeze.

"Are you ready to go, my American floozie?"

"Sure. Let's go, *tight arse.*"

Chapter 3

SAM

We spent the rest of the night hanging out with old and new friends, sending messages back and forth to our immediate family. We kept glancing around, trying to figure out if the woman from the bathroom was still at the pub, but thankfully, no one ever approached Hugh.

I kept getting text messages from my family back in California. Apparently, everyone knew about the proposal beforehand. I barely had the time to send a group text before everyone in my family chimed in with messages, GIFs, and wishes for a long life together. Even my brother Rob—who'd been skeptical about love and relationships since our parents' marriage crumbled—seemed to be really excited for me.

"I can't believe you asked my dad," I told him,

incredulous, staring at his eyes that seemed to sparkle even in the dim light of the pub.

He breathed out a laugh and shrugged. Then, his smile grew bigger, and his eyes seemed even brighter.

"It was the right thing to do." He bit his bottom lip, and that made me want to kiss him again, but I didn't want to encourage our rowdy friends to make fun of us some more. Throughout the evening, any time our lips would touch, they'd cheer and whistle.

Just a little while before, they'd caught us coming out of the bathroom together. True to form, Cecilia started singing "Hands to Myself" by Selena Gomez just as she'd promised.

Hugh turned a bright red and tried to downplay his embarrassment with an easygoing smile. Blood rose to my cheeks as well, but because of my skin tone, I was able to hide it better. While I really didn't care about people whistling and cheering at us, Hugh looked a bit uncomfortable—or maybe I was imagining things. Maybe it was just a combination of the alcohol, our bathroom encounter, and the uproar of emotions we were both navigating through.

Still, even slightly flustered, he looked so beautiful, so *happy*, and he was happy because of me. I still couldn't believe this man was mine and that he wanted to spend the rest of his life with me. After what I'd gone through with Eric, I had been determined to steer away from love, but falling for Hugh had been entirely too easy.

Everything about him was intoxicating and no matter how hard I tried, I couldn't resist him. Since Hugh and I had reconnected back at the Oscars, I often fantasized about marriage. I thought it would be something we'd discuss, eventually.

His proposal had undoubtedly shocked me, and part of me worried it might be a bit too soon. But, another bigger part of me—the part that still somehow believed "love conquers all"—knew I shouldn't be second-guessing what I felt.

He was it for me, and I knew he loved me as much as I loved him, though I wasn't completely sure why.

"When did you talk to him?" I leaned in and looked up at his face, inhaling his heavenly scent, a mix of peppermint and something woodsy. It was the same scent I'd caught in the cottage. As my mind went to our home, I envisioned exploring and christening every corner of the place. Frolicking with him around the glen couldn't come soon enough. I had been fantasizing about it since the year before.

"A few months ago, when we were back in LA, I also talked to your mother, too, ye ken . . . since your parents are divorced."

I laughed nervously. "You really thought of everything, didn't you?" I asked, my voice colored with surprise. Going from a cheating boyfriend who wouldn't commit to one who worshipped you and laid the grounds for your life together was quite the change.

"I bet my mom loved that you asked her."

"You're right about that, *mo chridhe*. She was thrilled. But, you see, I wasn't much worried about your parents or your family . . . there was just one person who knew that I was worried about. I thought for sure she'd end up telling you and ruin the surprise."

"Who could you possibly be talking about, I wonder?" I asked, raising my eyebrows.

He exhaled a deep breath and winked. We both turned in the direction of my former roommate, who was mingling around with some of the other makeup artists from last year. "Cecilia, always the troublemaker." I smiled.

"Your sister, too," he added, his accent a bit heavier on the last word. "She was so excited, for a moment there I regretted telling her."

"My sister?"

"She can't wait to help you plan this wedding, apparently."

"Mira? Help out? When would she ever find the time?"

"I dinna ken, but she said if we want to get married in LA, she knows people who could help out."

I shook my head. "I'd rather keep this wedding and us as far away from all that Hollywood madness as possible." I sighed. The more I tried to imagine a wedding in LA, the more I despised the idea, and as I looked around the pub and all the familiar faces, I knew it wasn't what I wanted.

"I want to get married here." There was no hint of doubt in my voice, and when my eyes met his, I noticed them grow softer. He held his bottom lip between his teeth and exhaled. Then, the soft look was replaced by one full of mischief.

"You want to get married here? Here at the pub?" he joked, and I swatted him on his *tight arse*.

"No, silly, but I do want to get married here in Scotland. Besides, you in a kilt in the hot LA weather? I just can't picture it." I stifled a yawn.

"We should be getting back, Sam. You must be tired.

A Scottish Wedding

Did you not get to sleep on the plane?" His brows furrowed, his mesmerizing blue eyes studying my face.

"I couldn't sleep—I was too excited to see you."

He cradled my face in his hands and pressed his lips to mine.

I closed my eyes, lost in the moment, deciding to ignore everyone around us. I wrapped my arms around his neck and kissed him back with all I had, not caring one bit about the cheers and claps coming from our loud, drunk friends.

Except for my new house and my hot new roommate, season two was set to begin the same way as season one. The actors were going to resume their training, and the production team was going to have meetings for each department and schedule ahead for the next few weeks. We would start shooting in a couple of weeks.

Last year, when I'd gotten there, I was nervous and worried I wouldn't be up to the task after working on the set of a TV comedy.

This year, I was worried for a few different reasons.

And just like the previous year, I couldn't sleep.

To be honest, I wasn't sure how much of my insomnia was due to jetlag and how much was first-day jitters. But, once awake, I knew I was going to have the hardest time going back to sleep and instead of tossing and turning in bed, I decided to go for what I knew would relax me while my man was sound asleep.

Baking.

Baking would ease my nerves. As I started thinking about work again, the uneasy feeling in my stomach became more pronounced. I knew I had no reason to be worried, but I couldn't help myself. I felt a bit guilty toward my coworkers. Hugh and I had been forced to keep things under wraps, and besides a handful of people, no one knew about us.

Then I was let go, and everyone soon found out about the real reason: I was let go *because* Hugh and I were seeing each other.

Since I had gotten back, I had seen some of the crew, but not everyone I had worked with. I wondered how they'd take the fact that I was back, and now *engaged* to the star of the show. Everything had happened so fast, and Hugh and I had been so desperate to be with each other during the last couple of days, we hadn't even talked about the wedding yet. I glanced around the cottage, astounded he'd been able to get the whole place renovated in just a few months. Clearly, the man had plans for us.

I would have gone to the courthouse if it had been just the two of us—was it even called that in Scotland?—but I wanted my family and his to be present.

Wedding scenarios started filling my head, fantasies of white dresses, kilts, images of Hugh's niece and nephew, Claire and Rory, running around on a green hill. I'd have loved to have an outdoor wedding, but with Scotland's moody weather, it would have been suicidal. I mixed the batter for the cookies I was making with a spoon—I hadn't had the chance to equip my fancy kitchen with small appliances. I was so lost in my thoughts, I didn't hear him come downstairs.

"What are you up this early for?" Hugh asked, his frame filling the narrow staircase of the cottage as he came down.

"Did I wake you? I didn't mean to. I was trying to be quiet."

"No, you didn't wake me." His eyes were weary, taking in the mess crowding the kitchen. He placed a kiss on my forehead and then gave me an inquisitive look. "What are you doing, Sam?" he asked, hands on his hips, his beautiful face marked by a deep frown. I let out a chuckle, because when he spoke with his serious, deep voice, he made me stupid. He eyed me with an air of curiosity and I finally fessed up.

"I'm making cookies for everyone. Tomorrow's a big day." It would be our first day back on set, and I wanted to do something nice for the crew.

"Sam, you know people don't expect you to feed them all the time."

"I know, but . . ." Cecilia and I had hosted quite a few get-togethers the year before, and I honestly didn't mind cooking for people. It gave us an opportunity to socialize and made those first few weeks in St. Martin less lonely.

He stared at me, his eyebrows drawing closer together as his frown deepened.

"You're nervous."

"Yes." I let out a deep breath and instantly felt the biggest part of the weight on my chest lift. Yes, I had seen people here and there around town, but the next day would be the first day back on set, and there were so many coworkers I still hadn't seen since I'd left in January.

"It's just first-day jitters," he offered with a shrug and a kind smile.

"Is it really, though?"

"Well, what else would it be?" he asked, eyebrows pulled together as he reached out for one of my banana peanut butter cookies. "You know everyone. You know what's expected of you. You're even familiar with the 'drop-dead gorgeous male lead who's stealing hearts left and right.'" He grinned at me, and I had to laugh because I knew he was quoting one of the headlines we'd read together in a recent magazine.

The corners of his lips rose and he smiled at me in that certain way that made my heart swell. I smiled back, but hastily took the cookie away from him and he made a face.

"Come on, can't you even spare one?" he protested.

"Wait a moment. It's missing something." I reached for a scoop of Nutella buttercream frosting and coated the cookie with it.

"So, why do you feel so nervous, Sam?"

"I don't know. I feel kind of . . . guilty."

My eyes met his blue depths. Earlier, they had reminded me of the Scotland sky on a sunny day, but now they were a bit clouded. He looked equal parts intrigued and confused.

"What do you have to feel guilty about?"

"Well . . . me . . . and you."

"What do you mean?"

"I mean that I worked side by side with most of these people for months and they never knew about . . . us, and even when I got fired, I still didn't tell them. They had to find out afterward. I mean, if that were me . . . I would feel

A Scottish Wedding

a little betrayed, that's all."

He placed the cookie down and started laughing at me. His laugh was quiet as a whisper at first, and then grew louder and wouldn't stop. He was laughing so hard that he was clutching the corners of the marble countertop.

"Come on! It's not funny."

"It is," he said in his Scottish accent.

His accent seemed to be heavier on the most random words. He was a trained actor, and he could speak with a perfect British accent, or even American when required, but in daily life, traces of Scottish slang and accent made welcome appearances. I loved when he rolled his Rs, and when the tone of his voice went higher on the last word in a sentence. I'd heard him speak with an American accent during an interview on a dare, and the difference was startling, to say the least. His voice was still beautiful, but it felt like it was missing something. I liked every single part of my Scot, but the low rumble of his voice and his accent were two of the things that simply drove me crazy.

"Samhain, do you really think anyone is going to hold a grudge because you kept our relationship a secret? They knew we had no choice." He tilted his head in my direction and I let out a sigh.

Maybe he was right. I was probably overreacting, just as I had the year before when I started working on *Abarath*. Back then, I was a ball of nerves and insecurities—insecurities that came from the fact that I'd been cast away from Hollywood following my very public revenge on my cheating boyfriend. Also, I had been working on a TV show that didn't pose many challenges makeup-wise, and *Abarath* had a heavy amount of prosthetics, fake blood, and special effects involved.

For weeks, I felt I really didn't deserve to be there, and even more so when I replaced the main makeup artist, Margaret, and started working directly with the main lead.

My fiancé.

"You know you have nothing to worry about. It wasn't your fault, or mine; it was just how things had to be. Thank God that's over," he said with a deep sigh. I knew keeping things secret had been as hard for him as it had been for me. The network behind *Abarath* wanted to milk the chemistry between Hugh and one of the female leads, Melissa, but neither one of them were interested in prolonging the charade. Hugh and I were falling in love, and there was also the fact that Melissa was gay. After his very public declaration of love at the Vanity Fair Oscar party, the network didn't have a choice but to back off for good.

Of course, there was a small price to pay.

After some photographers from the party came forward with pictures of Hugh serenading me at the Oscars, he had to agree to have them published.

The old saying "any publicity is good publicity" still rang true in Hollywood.

"No more worrying about what your colleagues are going to think, okay?"

"You're right, you're right, I know you're right," I said with a smile, quoting one of my favorite lines from *When Harry Met Sally*.

He smiled and finally took a bite of the Nutella-frosted cookie. His eyes lit up as he munched on the first bite, and a chorus of "Mmmmmm" followed.

I laughed. Sometimes watching him eat something I'd

made was as gratifying as eating itself. With the second bite, he added in an "Oh my God!" while rolling his eyes and succumbing to the deliciousness. He licked his thumb clean of the frosting he'd gotten all over it, adding a few more moans while he was at it.

"Hugh MacLeod! You better not orgasm on my cookies without me!" I yelled.

He covered his mouth with one hand, trying to finish his bite and stop himself from laughing at the same time, but I knew he couldn't help himself from being *vocal*.

The cookies were the bomb.

The banana and peanut butter gave the cookie a unique, balanced flavor, but it was the chocolate hazelnut frosting that took the recipe to a whole other level. It had been what I called a "happy accident" type of recipe after I messed up the consistency for muffins, and it was one I had been perfecting over the last couple years.

Needless to say, it had become a favorite in my family.

I opened the fridge and poured him a glass of almond milk. I placed it in front of him, he nodded his gratitude, and he drank half the glass then placed it back on the counter and grabbed a paper towel to wipe his mouth.

He circled around the counter and his hands wrapped around my waist from behind. Just the nearness of him made the hair on the back of my neck stand up, and it was even worse when he started whispering sweet nothings in my ear.

"How about I help you finish up here and then I give your sweet muffin something to moan about?" he asked, his voice low and seductive. Granted, the words were decidedly corny, but they were still effective. My throat went dry, and my body reacted in the way it always did when he tried to seduce me. He didn't have to try that hard, but the anticipation his words and touch ignited made foreplay a whole lot sweeter. A shiver ran down my spine, my breasts felt suddenly fuller and heavier, and wetness started pooling in my underwear. I couldn't see his eyes, but I would have bet anything I owned that the smolder was on full blast.

I turned around and my hands caressed his strong arms, his shoulders, all the way up to his neck. I ran my fingers through his soft, wavy hair and reached for his lips, thirsty for him.

"How about you forget about helping me in the kitchen and you help out elsewhere?" I asked, my voice loaded with need. He arched one eyebrow in response and leaned down just slightly so he could better reach behind my legs and lift me up. I didn't know what he had in mind, but I had learned in the last few months to just go with it. When it came to sex, the man was a constant surprise. He knew how to be sweet and slow, fast and rough, and I could never seem to get enough. As cliché as it sounded, when we were together, everything else disappeared. We existed only for each other. We might as well have been the last two lovers left alive, because in those moments, we couldn't seem to be bothered or distracted by anything else. Since most of the counter was occupied by the dozens of cookies I'd baked, he placed me on the opposite side of the stove, on the counter space between it and the sink. With a quick swoop, he took off my sweatshirt. I was naked underneath, and my nipples pebbled as the cool air washed over my skin.

The fiery look of determination coming from his icy blue eyes was devastating. It made me forget everything else. In that moment, only he mattered.

"Sam," he murmured, but didn't add anything else. He was too busy taking me in as his hands started tracing my skin and the swell of my breasts as if it were the first time all over again. I bit my bottom lip as he pinched one of my nipples, and I arched my back. I wrapped my legs around him and brought him closer to me. I loved the feel of his firm ass under my hands, and I loved the feel of his hard length against my needy, achy center even more.

I wanted him right then, but he seemed to have other ideas.

Chapter 4

HUGH

Her skin was always such a trigger for me, soft and warm, with that inviting caramel color that made me crazy. I started trailing kisses down her neck, reaching her collarbone. I lowered my head to kiss her breasts. She let out a low moan as I took a nipple in my mouth, and I sucked and licked just to hear her breath become fast and shallow. Her hands were in my hair, pulling me back so she could kiss me. She took my mouth with hers and her tongue wrapped around mine, giving me the sweet taste of her. I could taste chocolate on her tongue, tinged with a bit of coffee.

"I need you," she moaned as she broke the kiss.

"I'm here, *neach gaoil*," I said against her lips.

She hooked her fingers in the waistband of my trousers and pulled them down, along with my underwear. Her hand was on my erection right away, pumping it slowly as she brought her eyes up to mine.

I caressed her breasts as I looked into her chocolate brown eyes. It never failed to amaze me how those eyes could make me feel so many different things: love, lust, excitement, and a sense of familiarity.

I lost and found myself in them.

My hands skimmed the soft skin of her waist, and I dodged the fabric of her yoga pants to get to the place I liked to get lost in.

"Dammit," I muttered under my breath.

"What?" she asked in a husky voice.

"I should have taken your pants off first," I joked.

"I can get off the counter," she replied.

"No. Don't move."

She gave me a quizzical look. "I don't know what you have in mind, my dear Scot, but I'm not playing Cirque du Soleil with you." I laughed at her words, thinking about our first time in the trailer, when I hooked her on my shoulders and her head bumped against the ceiling. She scowled at me, and I took my shirt off.

That always seemed to distract her.

I knew my body turned her on as much as hers did me. I loved seeing that look of lust in her eyes, seeing the most passionate, fiery side of her come undone.

"Sam," I said. "Trust me. Hands up on the cabinets. Use the strength in your arms to lift yourself up. It will only take a moment. Stretch your legs out."

"Seriously?" she groaned. "Next time I'll get undressed before you put the moves on me."

I raised my eyebrows and let out a small laugh. "I don't

think you'll ever hear me complain about that." Despite her protestations, she did as I asked, and in one swift move, I pulled down both her pants and knickers and threw them on the floor.

"See? Now was that so hard?" She lowered her hands down on the counter again, but I shook my head and placed them up where they had been a moment ago.

She let out a small groan, but when I tugged on her ponytail and leaned down to kiss her, all humor was gone from her eyes.

"Get ready. Keep your hands up." I saw her swallow, and I knelt in front of her. I lifted her butt cheeks so she was right on the edge of the counter, ready and exposed to me. I parted the lips of her pussy with a finger. It was warm and so wet, and I couldn't wait to lose myself in it. Ever since we'd gotten back together and made it official, Sam and I made sure we were both clean. She'd decided to get on birth control so we could ditch the uncomfortable but necessary condoms, and being able to come inside of her was a brand new sensory experience. It was like a drug I could never get enough of.

"Ohhhh," she moaned as I licked her sweet pussy with my tongue. I parted her lips wider and started teasing and sucking her clit. "Oh, Hugh," she moaned as one of her hands caressed my hair.

"Hands *up*, Sassenach."

"Sorry, sorry," she mumbled. "God, you are . . . *ah*, so good at this. I can't . . . I can't . . . I'm going to come," she said.

"Don't hold back, Sam. Let go. Let me see you come," I said, looking up. She gave me a small nod, her cheeks a

A Scottish Wedding

shade darker than usual with a barely visible blush. I brought my face down to her again and licked and sucked her wetness, focusing on her throbbing clit. Her orgasm followed soon after, and I sucked her sweet, watery cum as she reached her climax in a chorus of low moans.

"You taste so fucking sweet, *mo gradh*," I told her, kissing her neck as she came down from her high. Her eyes were wide and her breath shallow. She searched for my mouth and kissed me, over and over.

"I want you," she murmured. "Take me. Now."

I cocked an eyebrow. "Don't have to tell me twice."

I lifted her legs again slightly and with a slow, deep thrust, I made my way into her.

"Ohhh, fuck," she said, her arms hooked around my neck as I held her legs under her knees and pushed in and out of her, keeping a slow tempo. I wanted to enjoy this as long as I could, but it felt so fucking good, I already knew I wasn't going to last very long.

"You feel so fucking good, Sam. You're perfect for me. Will you marry me?" I joked.

She laughed, and I loved feeling the sound of her laughter against my ear and her body vibrating around my cock. I drove into her harder and she answered with a strangled moan.

"I thought we already established that." She laughed.

"When?" I whispered. "When do you want to get married?" I asked.

"My my, Hugh MacLeod, I didn't know you to be the impatient type."

"Don't make fun of my love for you, Sam."

She met my eyes and gave me a small peck on the lips

as I drove into her once again.

"I would never do that. I'd marry you tomorrow if I could." I kept one of my hands under her knee, keeping her leg in place as I pumped into her, while the other caressed her breast, pinching her nipple. She arched her back and moaned as I drove into her a little deeper. She was so fucking sexy. I couldn't get enough of seeing her come apart.

"Yeah? You'd marry me tomorrow?"

"You know I would. I love you."

"I love you, too," I replied. "Fuck," I muttered. "Fuck, I'm going to come."

"Come, my love. Give it to me harder. Give me all you got."

I thrust into her three more times before I came, and as the orgasm erupted through my body, I had to hold on to my Sam to collect my bearings, panting hard, knees wobbly, beads of sweat dripping down my forehead. Sam brushed a lock of hair to the side and kissed my face over and over.

It was only then that I realized we were naked in the middle of the kitchen, surrounded by cookies and chocolate frosting.

I started laughing, still trying to catch my breath.

"What is it?" she asked in a curious tone.

"If this is what they call 'domestic bliss,' sign me up."

She waved her left hand at me, the engagement ring sparkling on her finger.

"Looks like you're all signed up." She smiled, and I felt the urge to kiss her again and hold her in my arms for a wee bit longer.

"So, you'd marry me tomorrow?"

She nodded. "You know I would, but Fiona would have

A Scottish Wedding

our asses whipped with a paddleboard if we did that, and it would probably break my dad's heart, although he would never tell me that."

"True." She was right. We needed our families by our side. It wouldn't be the same without them. When it came to love, I'd always been cautious, but since meeting Sam, I'd discovered a more impulsive side of me I hadn't known I possessed. What I felt for her was raw and true. Sometimes, it made me feel a little reckless.

It was a feeling I'd grown to embrace.

"I want to marry you, soon—the sooner the better—but we need to plan it, and tomorrow we start working on season two. You know you need to give it one hundred percent, so let's take it one day at a time, okay?" she said gently.

The smile on my face fell, although I knew she was trying to do what was best for us. She kissed me again and wrapped her arms tightly around my chest as the door busted open and a gust of wind blew through the house.

SAM

What I'd said about Hugh and I getting lost in each other to the point we wouldn't know what else was happening? Yeah, that happened often, and now Cecilia was waltzing through our living room, calling our names.

"Did you leave the door unlocked?" I whispered to my fiancé.

"I might have," he admitted.

"Hugh!" I said, slapping his arm. Cecilia was seconds

away from coming to look for us in the kitchen, where we were still butt naked.

"Sam and Hugh, it's time to wake up! Come down!" My pest of a friend had come all the way out to the valley to bother us. I wondered why she wasn't curled up with her own guy on such a fabulous Sunday.

"We are awake," Hugh said, peering at her over the kitchen's bar, which was covered in piles of cookies. From where she was, she could only see him waist up. I put my sweatshirt on, and I noticed him stretch out his arm. "Stop right there. We're naked, so don't come forth. Turn around Cecilia," he told her, and the assertiveness in his voice sounded so damn sexy.

Ahhh, this man, I thought to myself.

"Ewww! I didn't need the visual. Thanks a lot, McHottie. Now I'm going to spend the rest of my day trying to erase the image of you two shagging surrounded by baked goods. Pretty sure that's a food safety violation."

"Hush!" I yelled. "Next time don't go barging into someone's home," I told her as I put my pants on.

Cecilia muttered something else under her breath, but when I was finally dressed and peeked in the living room, I noticed she'd turned around and was facing the fireplace.

I checked to make sure my man was fully dressed, and then I walked into the living room and tapped my spunky friend on the shoulder.

"Now, care to tell me why you're here?"

Chapter 5

SAM

"Oliver and I are going to get married at the town hall this Friday. We got permission to take off. Actually, we persuaded Nora to give us a *half*-day off."

"Excuse me? You persuaded Nora to give you a half-day off to get married? It's the first week of season two—what methods did you use? Blackmail? Torture?"

She made a face and rolled her eyes. "What do you Americans say? Ahh, that's right . . . *Bitch, please.*"

I stuck my tongue out in response. It wasn't that the show runner, Nora Peters, was such a hard-ass—well, maybe sometimes she was—but she was dedicated to her job and made no concessions to anyone.

Abarath was her baby. She would usually let nothing and no one disrupt shooting schedules. She hadn't been one to oppose the relationship between Hugh and me last year, but she certainly was on the fence about it, mainly because she didn't want it to compromise or affect the success of the show.

"No, seriously—how did you get her to agree to give you time off?"

"Well, for one, it's the first week, and we haven't even started shooting yet. Two, there's some major Scotland vs. England rugby match every bloke from the crew is *dying* to go to. It's in Edinburgh, and they had already been asking her about working a half-day on Friday. It just worked out that way."

"That's right, the rugby match," said Hugh, as if he were suddenly remembering something. "Now I remember the guys talking about wanting to go."

I raised my eyebrows, surprised by the sudden interest, since the subject hadn't come up, not one time in all the months we'd been together. But, it would have to wait, because I had more pressing questions to ask.

"Wait, Cecilia, you're getting married this Friday? At the town hall? Are you sure that's what you want?"

"Sam!" Hugh said in a reprimanding tone.

What did I say?

"What? I thought she wanted a big wedding!" I said with a shrug. "I figured you wanted something more . . . traditional, that's all."

She shrugged but gave me a dreamy smile, which made me understand she didn't care about what I'd just said. "Oliver and I don't care," she said with a sigh. "To be honest, we're trying to save up. We want to buy a place in the country."

A Scottish Wedding

"Oh. That sounds nice," I told her, raising my eyebrows. "So, you're sure you don't want a big, puffy dress?" I joked, and she shook her head.

"What about a four-tier cake?"

"Oh, we'll have cake—maybe not quite four-tier, but there's going to be a celebration, at the pub, obviously."

"Obviously."

"So, you two already have your license?" Hugh asked, arms folded in front of his chest, his right hand holding his chin.

"We do! We got it the week before last, before both of you got here," she replied, turning toward Hugh. Her hair had gotten longer in the past few months. It was just as blond as when she had it short, but now it reached her shoulders. Her hair was straight, but with wavy strands. Every time she turned between Hugh and me, her hair whipped back and forth. I pondered her words and studied her demeanor, finally realizing how excited she really was about all this. It made my stomach fill with butterflies.

My friend was getting married—in just a few days.

"Why haven't you said anything?"

"What do you mean? I came as soon as I knew. We wanted to make sure we had Friday off."

"Yeah, but you could have mentioned something," I said in a slightly annoyed tone. Hugh narrowed his eyes at me, almost glaring. Was I really that out of line? "I'm just surprised, that's all, but it doesn't matter, okay? What can I do to help you?"

Hugh's eyes softened then, and I nodded in his direction. *I get it, okay?* I wanted to tell him. I wasn't trying to be an ass, but Cecilia had shocked me a little bit.

Knowing how exuberant she was in day-to-day life, I'd expected someone like her to dream of an over-the-top *Four Weddings and a Funeral* type of British wedding with a big party where all the attendees wear those fancy hats like the ones you see the royal family wear.

"Well, we would like for both of you to be there, if possible, as our witnesses."

Hugh and Oliver hadn't been particularly close when I was there the year before, but supposedly they had bonded after I had to leave, when Hugh was nursing his broken heart and I was dealing with my own heartbreak thousands of miles away. Plus, I suspected the only other viable candidate for such a task was Rupert, and knowing him, he was probably going to the game.

"Of course, I would love to do that!" I said, stretching my arms out to hug her. She embraced me and I held her petite frame for several seconds before I released her. "Anything else you need?"

"Do you think you could do my makeup? I'm afraid my hands will shake so bad I'll mess it up."

I smiled. "Of course, Cece. I would love to. I'll do anything you need me to."

I was welcomed back on set with opened arms. Just like Hugh said, I had nothing to worry about, but the rules for the two of us *were* a bit different this year.

When we got our schedule for the week, we noticed we

had a meeting scheduled with Human Resources.

Together.

Some HR person from London had been sent over to address a few things before season two started. Cecilia and Oliver had also been summoned, apparently, because I saw their name written down on a list in front of the HR representative.

Since everyone knew about us, we'd have to work harder to prove we were being professional and weren't fooling around on set.

Tsk.

Honestly, I didn't even know what they were complaining about—we had never delayed production during season one . . . except maybe *one or two* times when Hugh couldn't keep his hands to himself.

So, this year the mandatory rule for the star of the show was that under no circumstance would he get his makeup done in his trailer as he'd previously requested, unless he was sick as a dog.

He would have to go to the makeup room like everyone else, just like we had at the beginning of season one.

Nora took us aside on the very first day. "I don't care what you do after hours, but if you hold up production for *any reason*, you'll have to deal with me," she told us with a loaded, menacing look.

I knew Nora well enough to know only a fool would dare crossing her.

HUGH

A few days later, we found ourselves sitting in the Registrar's office, ready to act as witnesses for Cecilia and Oliver's wedding.

Sam was staring at our hands laced together.

"You know, I never thought this would be something I'd want, but now that we're here . . ." Sam's voice trailed off and when her eyes met mine, she gave me a soft, shy look. There was hesitation and emotion in her voice. I hadn't brought the subject up again because I knew we were both too busy to make it happen any time soon.

But that didn't mean I hadn't been thinking about it.

The fact that we were just about to witness our friends exchange vows only made the desire, the need to make her my wife stronger.

I grinned at her. Her words and her shy hesitation made me smile.

"Have you changed your mind?"

"Maybe . . . but I would prefer it if our families could be present."

"I know." I nodded and she let out a deep breath.

"I'm excited for Cecilia and Oliver, though."

The bride and groom were sitting on a bench in front of us, waiting for their turn. I glanced at my fiancée and noticed a look of nervousness and trepidation in her eyes. She kept pressing her lips together as she often did when she didn't want to succumb to her emotions. I'd watched her try to hold back tears many times when we watched movies or TV shows. I clearly remembered how distraught she'd

A Scottish Wedding

looked when we watched a certain episode of *Abarath* together. I wasn't too keen on watching myself on screen, but in this particular episode they'd asked us to live-tweet the show, so I'd watched it with Sam and her family while it aired in the US.

It was an episode I remembered well, because it was when it all started, when I started falling for her. I was terribly nervous to shoot a very dramatic scene that day, and she'd found me in my trailer, unable to get a bloody grip on myself.

With just a few words, she'd been able to remind me that I could do it. In that moment, she'd given me the confidence I had been missing.

When we'd watched the scene that had cemented our connection and brought us together, tears streamed down her cheeks just as they had that day on set. I'd wiped her tears and kissed her cheek while we watched the show. She had bashfully pursed her lips, trying to downplay her feelings.

Similarly, now that we were waiting for Cecilia and Oliver to exchange their vows and preparing to act as their witnesses, she seemed to be on the verge of tears.

"Sam, what's up?" I asked, tugging on her hand.

She took a deep breath and exhaled slowly.

"I don't know, babe," she said in a whisper. "It's all of this. It's making me think about us, our wedding. I want it *now*, so much that I'd be ready to go through with it the same way they are, but I also want everything else. Is that wrong of me?"

She looked my way, eyes questioning, and I shook my head.

"Well then, if you want everything, we better start putting the wheels in motion."

"What do you mean?" she whispered.

"I hope you won't think I'm crazy, but I have a sort of crazy idea."

SAM

The very last thing you'd expect when you finally find the one and decide to get married is to get bitch-slapped in the face with a load of bureaucratic bullshit.

Seriously. *Major buzzkill.*

But that's just what happened to us.

Right after the Registrar declared Cece and Oliver husband and wife, Hugh told me all about his crazy idea.

"We might not want to get married right now, but we could get a license, or at least look into getting one."

And that's what we did.

Yes, he was right—it sounded crazy, but why not at least check out what we needed to do in order to get one?

We ran to the marriage license office, jubilant with excitement. He kissed my hand as we both laughed and knocked on the door.

Theoretically, it should have been simple, right?

Only, it wasn't.

Since I was a US citizen, I was supposed to have a visa in order to get married. I had a work visa, but that wasn't enough. I tried listening to the clerk going through the list of paperwork needed, but at some point, during out impromptu visit, my brain checked out and I stopped

A Scottish Wedding

listening.

It was all noise to me.

This was not what I wanted to hear, and from the tight hold Hugh had on my hand, I could tell he wasn't happy either. I thought I was just supposed to sign a paper, get something that would make it possible to record our union at the Registrar first and in a church later on. My eyes kept bouncing between the clerk's detached expression and the list of documents he pointed at on a form he'd placed in front of us.

More than anything else, I couldn't bear the look on Hugh's face. I barely glanced at him, and immediately I felt my heart ache. He looked just as shocked and as confused as I felt. After briefly locking eyes with me, he gave me a forced, small smile. It hurt to see him this disappointed, jaw taut, eyes narrowed, thick eyebrows pulled together in a frown.

I squeezed his hand and pulled it toward me, and another smile appeared on his face, still tight, but less forced than the one a moment before.

One of his hands reached around my waist and rested on my hip, heavily.

I could feel him steadying himself by leaning on me, physically and emotionally. I swallowed past the knot in my throat as my heartbeat sped up and the blood coursed through my body faster. Looking at him, I was reminded of all the reasons why I loved him.

This wasn't what we wanted to hear.

But we'd deal with this, too, because this love of ours knew no barriers.

Nothing was going to stop us, least of all a long list of

paperwork.

In that moment, a small spark lit within me.
Whatever it took, I was going to make it happen.
For *him*.
For *us*.

HUGH

"So, that wasn't at all what I expected," I said nervously after a while, letting out a deep breath. I was frustrated by what we'd been told at the Registrar's office and had been quiet since we left. Sam glanced at me from time to time as we walked hand in hand. We were going to join everyone else at The World's End, a historic pub in Edinburgh, which was just a short twenty-minute walk away. The guys who had gone to the rugby game were also supposed to meet us there, and then later we were scheduled to take the celebration back to St. Martin.

I was happy for our friends, but right at that moment, I didn't have it in me to celebrate. I didn't like having to hear what the clerk at the office had told us.

"I know." Sam sighed, and I realized she was probably just as confused and frustrated as I was. "But," she said, giving my hand a squeeze, "it's probably just a matter of getting things started. I'm sure we'll get everything sorted out soon."

"Maybe so," I replied with a small smile.

"I was thinking . . . you should put me in touch with your attorney. He can probably recommend a colleague or a friend who practices immigration law. We're both busy, and we're never going to have time to take care of this if we don't get someone experienced who can guide us through."

"You're right." I nodded, suddenly feeling more hopeful. The sun abruptly broke through the clouds and shined its afternoon golden glow on the centuries-old buildings that lined the street. The sunlight forced me to look up and take in all the different colors the city had to offer, bringing back so many memories from when I was in school.

"I had forgotten how much I love walking around Edinburgh," I said out loud without realizing it.

"It's beautiful," Sam chimed in. "I wish we could have visited more last year."

I nodded. She stopped in her tracks and pulled my hand up to her chest.

"Hugh, I'm disappointed too, but it's all going to work out, I just know it. It's just going to take a bit longer than we thought. Why don't you let me handle it?" She smiled tentatively, searching my eyes, and I realized how moody I had been for no reason.

I smiled. My Sam, she always knew how to help me put things into perspective.

I stepped closer to her, leaned in, and cradled her face. I looked around, and thankfully no one seemed to be paying attention to us. It was a Friday afternoon, and everyone was bustling to either get home or to the pub.

I locked eyes with her and her lips parted, anticipating a kiss. My finger traced the shape of her cheek, all the way down to her chin.

"You see, this is why I can't wait to marry you. You always make everything better, Sam." I placed a small kiss on her lips, and when I pulled back, she leaned in for another one.

"It's all going to work out. It's going to be epic, you'll see. Now, let's go and celebrate with our friends. No time for long faces." She tugged on my hand, motioning for me to follow her. "The World's End," she mumbled. "Why does it sound so familiar?"

"Probably because it's one of Edinburgh's oldest establishments. You might have heard someone else talk about it."

"I don't think so, I don't recall any conversation . . ." She trailed off. I glanced her way as her frown turned into sudden realization. "Of course! How could I be so stupid?"

"What?" I asked.

"The World's End!"

"What about it?"

"It's where Jamie and Claire go after their reunion in *Voyager*!" I gave her a look of confusion and she sighed, exasperated. "Hugh, remember Jamie Fraser from *Outlander*? Best book boyfriend, fictional husband, no-one-can-hold-a-candle-to-him, all-around badass hero?"

I raised my eyebrows in response, only a wee bit offended Sam didn't care for Abarath quite the same way.

"Don't give me that. We talked about this—Abarath is no Jamie Fraser. Different ballpark, MacLeod. Claire and Jamie's love story withstands time and space!" she tried to reason. "Maybe I will change my mind about him if he stops being such a damn *flirt*!" She wasn't wrong there; unlike Jamie Fraser, Abarath had no qualms about not being monogamous.

"Fine. You're right. Can we go now, lass? I'm ready for

a pint."

"Of course. Let's go," she said, taking my hand and leading the way. We walked for a few minutes, fingers laced together, and then she stopped in her tracks again.

"Um, Hugh . . . you should take the lead."

"Why is that?"

"Because I have no bloody idea where The World's End is."

I pursed my lips together, noticing how cute she sounded when she said *bloody*.

"Dinna fash yourself. I ken my away around here, *neach-gaoil*."

"Why is it called The World's End, anyway?"

"Because, once upon a time, that was where the city of Edinburgh ended. The walls of the city were just a few steps away, the world's end, ye ken. Everything outside those walls was foreign and dangerous—a bit like you, in a way," I told her with a smug smile.

"Har har," she replied, laughing and igniting a warm ache in the middle of my chest.

"You know what, though, Sam?"

"What?"

"I wouldn't want it any other way."

She smiled, the corners of her lips tipping up. She glanced at me, her eyes twinkling in the afternoon light.

"I wouldn't want it any other way, either," she replied softly.

Chapter 6

SAM

"Wake up, sleepyhead." I heard Hugh's heavy footsteps across the floor. He stopped in front of the window, the one facing east, and a few seconds later, daylight invaded the bedroom as he opened the curtains.

"Nooooo," I mumbled, putting a pillow on top of my head. I heard the muffled sound of his laughter, beautiful even though it was at my expense. I felt the weight of the mattress shift as he sat down on the edge of the bed.

"Come on, Sam. Get up. There's something I want to show you."

I patted the mattress. "You get back in here, now. I can show you things here, too. It's Saturday, for crying out loud, and we were out late last night. Let me sleep."

He took the pillow that was keeping me safe from the blinding daylight and brushed the hair away from my face.

A Scottish Wedding

I squinted, my eyes trying to adjust to the . . . brightness.

Oh, Scotland. It's so like you to be bright and sunny on one of the days I do not have to get up at dawn to go to work.

I grunted and the Scot laughed again.

I tried to put him in focus as his silhouette was bathed in daylight. He caressed my face, trailing the contour of my cheek.

I looked up and the irresistible grin I'd grown to love was plastered on his face. It was impossible to remain grumpy and serious when he looked at me like that. I took a deep breath and a warm ache radiated through my chest; it was the best kind of ache I'd ever felt.

"Come on, Sam," he said softly.

I clutched tightly on the sheet and the blanket, not ready to leave my cocoon. He was being sweet about it, but his insistence still pissed me off.

Then, the fragrant smell of coffee reached my nostrils. *At least he comes bearing gifts*, I thought, but then I looked to the bedside table and saw no cup of coffee greeting me.

So the coffee was downstairs, only accessible if I got out of bed.

This Scot was damn sneaky.

I grunted again, and eventually decided to give in.

I lifted the blankets and sat up, staring at him. I let out a deep breath.

"What's gotten you so worked up that you can't wait thirty minutes or an hour to wake me up?" I teased.

He gave me a flirty grin, the type I couldn't be indifferent to. His eyes were a cornflower blue this morning, especially with the bright sunshine entering the room, but what made me forget everything was the look in those eyes, his gaze serious, yet soft.

He took one of my hands in his and frowned as he looked down at our joined hands.

"You didn't use to be so lazy, Sam. What happened?" he asked, running his fingers on the inside of my wrist, tickling me with his soft touch. There was a hint of a smile on his face; he was kidding—thank God. "You used to be out there, taking in the fresh air."

I cleared my throat. "Uh, only when I was severely jetlagged or trying to escape Cecilia and Oliver."

"Well, come on. It's a beautiful day and there's something I want to show you. It's supposed to start raining later today, so we better enjoy the sunshine now."

"Of course," I replied sarcastically, and he laughed. Typical Scotland—when was it not raining or about to be raining? I could bet even local weathermen had the hardest time "predicting" the weather.

Unpredictability when it came to weather wasn't one of my favorite things about Scotland, but even if I wasn't accustomed to it yet—and maybe never would be—I was learning to tolerate it. After all, it was the unpredictability of the elements that contributed to making the scenery so unbelievably gorgeous.

I reluctantly got out of bed and watched him as he followed my every move with hooded eyes. I wondered if he knew I was deliberately going slow in the hope that he would just toss me on the bed and change his mind.

Yes, sunshine was nice and all, but nothing compared to a nice romp between the sheets. Hugh MacLeod beat sunshine every day; I didn't need vitamin D when I could have him.

Alas, he didn't touch me, and after a quick visit to the bathroom, I was fully dressed and ready to go.

At least he was nice enough to pour some coffee in a portable mug for me, and he had a backpack packed.

Where are we going?

He opened the door of the cottage and after he locked it, he took my hand in his.

I was surprised when we didn't head for the car.

We were in the middle of a valley, isolated from pretty much everything.

"We're not taking the car?" St. Martin was thirty minutes away.

"We're going on a hike."

He laced his fingers with mine and looked down at me, giving me a soft, knowing smile.

"What's this thing you want me to see?"

"Just a few more minutes."

I stared at him in disbelief, wondering what was up with him. The man could be full of surprises when he wanted to be. If there was something he thought I should see, maybe I should just get along with it and stop being so darn grumpy.

I took a sip of my coffee from the mug.

Mmmm. The warm coffee was an instant mood booster, and I decided to stop thinking about where we were going. I was going to find out in due time. I held the hand of my man tighter and walked alongside him.

A good ten or fifteen minutes into our hike, I could finally see what he'd been so insistent about, and it left me breathless.

So much so that I stopped dead in my tracks.

The heather was in bloom.

It wasn't just sporadic patches as when I'd arrived a couple of weeks before.

It was in full bloom, and almost the entire glen was covered with it.

"Oh, Hugh."

It was so beautiful, it brought tears to my eyes.

"It's beautiful, isn't it?"

"It's the most beautiful thing I've ever seen," I replied as a tear ran down my cheek before I could wipe it away. I tugged his hand and pulled him down to me.

"I love you," I told him, brushing my lips against his. "Let's go up there."

He smiled against my mouth.

"I knew you'd change your mind," he said with a soft laugh.

"You should have said something sooner, showed me what I was about to miss out on." I had to admit, I was a bit ashamed of how cranky I'd been.

"Let's go to our place," I said, stretching up on my toes to give him a kiss on the cheek.

We walked in silence for the rest of the time, me occasionally sipping my coffee, taking in the beauty of the place that a year before had completely stolen my heart.

I had been with Hugh the very first time I saw the heather in bloom on this glen, and I had been with him a few weeks later when I ventured into the valley on a bright, sunny day very similar to this one.

"Was it over here?" he asked. He didn't need to add more, because I knew what he meant. He was looking for

A Scottish Wedding

the exact spot where he'd found me sitting last year.

"I think it was somewhere around here," I said, taking a few more steps. "I remember I could see the cottage straight down from here." I took a seat in the heather and he joined a few seconds later.

He rested his strong arms on his knees and I rested my head atop one of his biceps.

A year before, I'd been sitting in that very spot thinking about the chaos that was my life, commiserating on the mess I'd made. I remembered looking at the cottage and thinking how peaceful and wonderful it would be to live there, surrounded by all this.

At the time, the man next to me wasn't even part of the equation, not because I didn't like him—in fact, my crush had been hard to keep at bay even then—but because it was so unlikely that he would feel about me the way I felt about him.

Actors were self-centered and fickle most of the time, at least in my own experience, but this man . . . he was the antithesis of selfish.

He'd made so many things happen for us. He'd fought for us to be together despite circumstances. He hadn't given up.

And now he was giving me the greatest happily ever after. Just thinking about everything he'd done for us left me overcome with emotion.

I wanted to give him everything. He deserved everything.

Ideas started brewing in my head, and in that moment, I didn't know just how or when, but I knew I had to make it happen.

He'd made me a promise, and I would deliver on it.

The knot that formed in my throat was hard to swallow. Tears pooled at the corners of my eyes, and I wiped them away.

"What is it?" he asked in a low voice, thick with his beautiful accent.

"Nothing," I replied. "I didn't mean to get sappy, but I guess I can't help it. It's just . . . you know, so many memories." I hesitated.

"I ken," he replied with a small nod and a grin. The look in his eyes told me he remembered everything. This place was special for us, not only because it was drop-dead gorgeous but because after we met out there in the heather, we had started falling for each other.

We'd gotten lost in each other in the best of ways.

"Hugh."

"What is it, Sam?"

"Last year, when we met up here . . . I wanted you to kiss me, so badly."

"I was *dying* to kiss you," he confessed, letting out a breath.

I laughed. "Why didn't you, then?"

"I don't know. I didn't want to come across as too forward, I guess." I frowned. "Also, we didn't have that many chances to talk, and I was enjoying getting to know ye."

"Always so sweet."

"It's the truth, lass," he said, and that made me smile. I leaned in to kiss him. It was a peck at first, but it grew into a deeper, longer kiss as his lips parted and his tongue searched for mine. I wrapped it around his eagerly, succumbing to the intensity of the moment, stroking and sucking until I was breathless.

"I want you," I pleaded, tugging on the zipper of his jacket.

"I'm yours," he replied simply.

"Now." My eyes were serious and full of intention, and when he met my gaze, his own eyes widened with a look of amusement as a stupidly delicious grin spread across his face. He glanced around and bit his bottom lip with a look full of mischief.

"I don't see why not. There's no one up here . . . let's do it."

Did he think his words were going to make me backtrack? Quite the contrary.

"Have your way with me, laddie." I took his hand and pulled him on top of me, feeling the weight of him as he covered me with his sculpted body.

"Is that a challenge or a plea, Sam?" he asked as he leaned down to kiss me.

"Both," I murmured, my voice low and needy against his lips.

I reached for the waistband of his pants, but he stopped my hand.

"Wait."

"Fuck no. You better not be teasing me with all your 'let's do it out here in the open' stuff."

"No, that's not what I meant. There's a blanket in the backpack."

"Oh."

"Yeah."

"Always so thorough," I replied with a shy smile.

He spread the small blanket on the ground next to us, inevitably smashing a bit of heather. It was a beautiful day in early August, and although it was sunny, the air was breezy, almost chilly. Still, nothing would have kept me from fooling around in the heather with my fiancé.

Hugh started trailing kisses on my neck, unzipping both my jacket and the lightweight fleece I was wearing underneath. His soft, feather-like, excruciatingly slow kisses were the best and the worst. My body arched and begged for him, my underwear already soaked with the promise of his hard length. I reached inside the waistband of his pants and grabbed his warm, hard cock in my hand, stroking him up and down as he let out a hiss.

He covered my chest with more kisses as he squeezed a breast in one hand.

"Have I told you how much I love zippers?" His voice was a low rumble, his breath so delicious, teasing my skin. Mixed with the chilly air, it caused my skin to break into goose bumps.

"There's one more," I teased, giving him a seductive look.

He stopped, balancing his weight on his elbows.

"Oh, good thinking, bra makers," he joked as he unzipped the front of my sports bra. I laughed and then drew in a deep breath as his tongue found its way to one of my nipples, licking and sucking hard.

One of his hands trailed inside my leggings, pushing aside the soaked underwear, finding my wet center.

"So wet," he murmured. My hand was still around his cock, but I stopped stroking him now that he was distracting me with his finger, pushing in and out of me as his thumb pressed down on my clit, causing my legs and my entire body to tense up.

"Take my pants off," I mumbled against his lips, heady with desire. I let go of my hold on him, reluctantly. He straightened himself up, sitting on his knees, and with a wicked gleam in his eyes, proceeded to take off my boots and pants. I was lying almost completely naked in the heather, in broad daylight, and somehow, I didn't care one damn bit.

"You're so fucking beautiful, Sam," he murmured, almost as if he were saying it to himself.

"As are you." I watched him with dreamy, lustful eyes as he leaned on top of me, anticipating what was about to happen. I struggled a bit to unzip his jacket. I needed to feel his body. My hand trailed underneath his Henley shirt and I roamed his warm skin, feeling his hard chest underneath my fingers. His lips reached for me, and I responded to his kiss, got lost in the taste of him as he parted my legs a bit wider to make room for himself. I lifted my hips and wrapped my legs around his waist. He positioned himself at my entrance and filled me with one thrust, making me moan against his lips.

He rocked his hips, filling me and stretching me as I arched my body under him. I couldn't help but moan his name softly as he thrust in and out, brushing against my sensitive spot over and over, driving me crazy. I opened my eyes and looked up as white, fluffy clouds moved above us, pushed by the breeze blowing in from the seaside.

His hands grabbed my backside, fingers kneading my skin, as if he couldn't get enough, as if he needed to get deeper, to own me even more than he did already.

He dragged his cock out of me slowly, thrusting in

again as deep as he could.

"Christ!" he muttered under his breath. "Samhain, I—"

"Don't stop. Don't stop. Don't slow down."

His eyes were full of determination, and I saw a flash of something I couldn't quite grasp. A moment later he gripped my hips tightly and rolled down on his back so I was suddenly straddling him. I let out a deep breath, adjusting myself now that I was on top.

He took advantage of the position, fondling my breasts as I moved up and down on his length at the same time he moved his hips, his cock creating the most delicious pressure on my clit, blissful yet maddening, so much it made me want to scream.

I moaned, hair falling on my face, and he brushed it away.

"Let me see you come, love," he said as he kept moving his hips faster and his cock filled me deeper and deeper. White-hot light flashed in my eyes, and my whole body tensed up around him as I cried out his name. He shook and grunted in a low voice underneath me as his hands caressed my ass. I leaned down on him, and he cradled my head as we both caught our breath, half naked in the valley lined with purple flowers.

"Did I fulfill your fantasy?" he teased.

I laughed softly. "Don't act like you haven't thought of this yourself," I replied.

"Oh, aye, I have—many times."

He took a deep breath and looked into my eyes before placing a slow kiss on my lips. I caressed his face and my eyes fell on my left hand, my ring sparkling as bright as his eyes under the sun.

He looked up at the sky and frowned. The clouds were moving faster now, and the wind had picked up.

He gave me a sly grin and another peck on the lips then lifted himself up so he was balancing on his elbows. "As much as I would like to lie naked in the heather with you, we better head back before the weather changes, Samhain," he said in a worried tone. I went along with it, though reluctantly.

I wasn't ready to leave our favorite place yet.

Chapter 1

Sam

In the end, he was right. The weather started changing rapidly as we made our way back to the cottage. The clouds covered the sun and turned from white and innocent to gray and ominous.

"Well, that was nice while it lasted," I muttered, looking up at the sky, and he laughed good-naturedly. A light, wet mist started coming down a few minutes later, and it soon turned into fat, heavy rain drops that caught up with us when we were still about fifteen minutes away from the cottage.

By the time we made it to the door, we were both soaked.

We opted to get in through the mudroom and shed our wet clothes there then we headed for the bathroom upstairs. I drew a bath and took off the remaining things I had on, namely my fleece and underwear. The uber-smart Scot had

had a state-of-the-art tub installed in our upstairs bathroom. Unfortunately, we never had the time to put it to good use. We were always running to and from work and never had the time for a bubble bath. It was time to christen it.

"Take off the rest of your clothes," I said as I started drawing a bath, making sure the water was the right temperature.

He didn't say a word, but his eyes sparkled with a naughty gleam.

I watched him take off his thermal Henley slowly, teasing me, putting on a show for me.

"Get in," I ordered him, pointing at the tub when he was naked in front of me.

His curly brown hair was wet from the rain, and I gently brushed it off his face.

He circled my wrist with his hand and pulled me closer to him.

"You get in now, lass," he said in a low, husky voice.

I did as he asked, and turned around when he motioned for me to sit on top of him.

I leaned back against his chest as the warm water soothed my cold, wet limbs.

"This tub was the best idea ever," I murmured against his neck before placing a soft kiss there. He caressed my face and kissed the top of my head.

"Better than the stove?"

"Shoot, I forgot about that other fab idea of yours. It's a toss-up between the stove and the tub," I said, thinking about the marvelous Viking Tuscany blue stove downstairs.

The stove was amazing, but sometimes I felt a bit

guilty. I didn't even want to think or argue about the price tag on that one. I'd attempted it before and knew it was pointless to bring it up again.

"Have you given any more thought to when you want to get married?" he asked, running his fingers up my arm and then across my stomach. I shivered at the touch and let out a sigh. We hadn't talked about it since our bubble got burst at the Registrar's office. I'd told Hugh I had no problem taking care of the paperwork and he'd put me in touch with his attorney, but I hadn't heard back from him yet. Maybe it was time to give him another call, especially after the fabulous idea I'd gotten while we were out on our hike.

I would have to make sure my Scot didn't suspect anything.

"I have," I said simply.

"And?"

"I want it to be soon, like you, but you need to give me time to get everything under control. Maybe start planning toward the end of our shooting schedule this season, and have it next summer."

"So, about a year from now?" he asked, and I couldn't help but notice the disappointment in his voice. I held on to the edges of the tub so I could turn around and look at him.

"Well, it really would be less than a year if we could get something planned for late spring or early summer. I meant what I said when Cecilia and Oliver got married, but give me time to pull it all together, okay? And, the other thing is . . . after I was so unceremoniously dismissed, I am concerned about doing a good job on set. I already have too many distractions as it is," I said, giving him a pointed look.

A Scottish Wedding

"Hmmm," he hummed, eyes sparkling with delight, fixed on my lips. Then, he frowned. "But, Sam . . . you know you didn't get fired last year based on your performance. You really shouldn't worry about that."

"Debatable."

"I'm serious," he said, and his accent was suddenly more marked. I smiled and kissed him on the lips.

"Still, I would like to be able to focus on what I need to do on a day-to-day basis without having to worry about planning a whole wedding."

"You know, I could help." The tone of his voice was low, his eyes dark, and his hand traveled from my collarbone down to my breast. He gave it a gentle squeeze then started teasing my nipple with his thumb and forefinger.

"Oh, really? Please do enlighten me. When would you even have the time to help?" I teased.

"I could find the time," he said as he brought my breast up so it was out of the water. He leaned down, sucked slow and hard on my nipple, making me lose my concentration. A few strokes of his tongue on my skin were all my pussy needed to become a tangled mess of nerves, aching for more attention from him.

"I could find the time," he repeated. "I have a few ideas already."

"What are these ideas? Please do share."

"There's a church in Stonehaven I have been to before, and I'd always thought that if and when I got married, I would like to do it there."

"Well, we need to figure something out. You're Catholic but I'm . . . well, I'm nothing, raised with no religion whatsoever. That's bound to raise some eyebrows, at least here in the old world," I teased.

"Come on, Samhain, you're overreacting."

"I'm serious. I am going to have to explain to whichever priest we speak to that neither my father or my mother cared to raise me according to any religion, even a nondenominational one."

"No one will care, you'll see."

"I have been trying to do some research, though, to see how it all works, you know."

"You have?" he asked enthusiastically.

"Yes. I haven't been to that many Catholic weddings, and I would like to be prepared a little."

"So, I know which church I want us to get married at, and you've been doing your research. All we need is to contact the priest, get your family airline tickets, and a dress for you."

"A dress for me—what about you? Do you think you're going to recycle one of your suits? No way."

"Who talked about recycling? I just need to find a new jacket and shirt, perhaps. I already have the bottom half," he said with a wink, and I laughed.

"That's right, you're going to wear your kilt, aren't you?"

He gave me a sultry look, and with a hand wrapped around my shoulder, he brought the other one down between my legs.

"That's right, and I plan to be traditional on our wedding day," he said in a seductive tone. He leaned over and gave me a peck, his tongue peeking between his lips, capturing mine slowly, wrapping around mine in a sensuous hold. I broke the kiss, heady and full of questions.

A Scottish Wedding

"Traditional?" I asked.

He raised one eyebrow. "Traditional, *neach gaoil*, when it comes the kilt."

"Ohhhh," I replied, raising my eyebrows in understanding. "Traditional, aye?"

"Aye," he said, running his nose along mine while his fingers made their way to my center, teasing my clit in a circular motion, putting just enough pressure on it to make me arch my back and ache for him to give me all of himself again.

"You're such a scoundrel," I told him in a shallow tone, my wits succumbing to my body's reaction. I enjoyed witty banter, but right now his touch was all I craved.

I found his hard length underwater and began stroking his smooth cock up and down.

"Sam, get on all fours."

"All fours?"

"Yes, lass. Grab the edge of the tub. I need to be inside you *now*."

Fuck me.

I gave him a sly look and did as he asked. He was rarely demanding in the bedroom, and I liked when he was. I wanted to play with him. I grabbed the edge of the oval-shaped tub, getting steady on my knees as I felt him rise out of the water behind me. I turned around slightly to look at his glorious body as ripples of water washed off his skin. He grabbed my hips, his erection hard against my back, and ran a finger up and down my slit. Grabbing his cock, he positioned himself at my entrance and pushed inside, hard and fast.

I gasped and grabbed the edge of the tub tighter.

He waited a moment before moving again, one hand on my hip, the other teasing my nipple. He thrust again, deep and slow, while his hand traveled across my stomach. He started moving steadily inside me, filling me so deeply I wanted to scream. It got worse—in the best possible way—when his hand met the entrance of my pussy and found my clit. His deep thrusts with his fast stroking of my center had me rocking my head backward, moaning his name, begging him to give me more.

"Harder, faster," I moaned—as if it were possible to feel even higher than what I felt right then. He kept a steady rhythm and I felt the orgasm burst through my body as I clenched around him, coming hard. He reached climax a couple seconds later, grasping the edge of the tub for balance with one hand, the other anchored around my waist. As the orgasm washed through him, he leaned his head on my back, breathing hard.

He pulled out, and before I could even straighten up, he bit my ass—*hard*.

"Ouch! That was a bit much, Mr. MacLeod." I turned to look at him, and he had the smuggest, most impenitent smile.

"I'm not sorry about that, Ms. Farouk." His grin lit up his whole face, and although I had planned to remain serious, I couldn't stop the smile stretching across mine.

Then, I had a sudden thought.

Am I going to change my name? Women in the US did it often, but I knew a lot of women in Europe kept their birth name.

We washed the soap off and got out of the tub just as the water was starting to get cold. I offered him a towel as I wrapped one around me.

The words slipped out of my mouth before I knew what I was saying.

"Am I going to change my name?"

He looked surprised, almost startled. He smiled warmly and bit his lip.

"When we get married, I mean."

"If you want to, but you don't have to do that."

"It wouldn't matter to you?" I asked. I couldn't deny that I was a bit surprised. Men seemed to always make such a big deal about the woman taking the husband's name.

"It doesna matter much to me, Sam. I can be traditional about some things and modern about others. Your name is part of your identity. As nice as it is to take your husband's name, I don't see it as necessary."

"Really?"

"Really. Whether you take my name or not, you'll be mine, to love and to cherish, till death do us part." I smiled at that, because he was right. Whether I decided to change my last name or not, I would be his. I was going to be his for the rest of my life.

Chapter 8

HUGH

I entered the makeup trailer at the end of our lunch break. Sam had told me she had some things to do and might have to skip lunch, so I was surprised to find her sitting with a bloke I had never seen before on the couch at the very end of the trailer.

They looked awfully cozy. The guy was wearing a nice light blue suit and Oxford shoes with brightly colored argyle socks. He certainly didn't look like a member of the crew; perhaps he was an employee from the network?

Sam was pointing out something on her iPad and gesturing animatedly, and he seemed to be taking notes on a tablet. Had I walked in on a meeting? If so, why was it only the two of them? Why were the other makeup artists not involved?

A Scottish Wedding

I took a few steps forward, making my presence known. Sam's head shot up, and an alarmed look appeared on her face before it was replaced by her sweet, reassuring smile.

What in the bloody hell is going on?

"What's going on here, Sam?"

"Hugh, this is Fern. He's the winner of the *internship*."

"Internship? What internship?"

"Oh, sorry. You probably haven't heard about it! Now that I think of it, it was an internal memo, crew only. Apparently, the network had a big contest a few months back. It was open to college students enrolled in movie-industry programs. Fern here is the winner of the internship for the makeup department, and he'll be on set with us for a couple hours a day, a few times a week."

"It's a pleasure to meet you, Mr. MacLeod. I'm such a huge fan of the show," Fern said, getting up and stretching his hand toward me.

"Nice to meet you too, Fern. Please call me Hugh," I told him, and the young bloke smiled sheepishly, as fans sometimes did, a red flush coloring his pale, almost translucent skin. His hair was styled in an unruly uppercut, his brown curls falling on the side of his face. He was a handsome chap, tall and lean, with startling pale gray eyes. His smile was wide, and his teeth were the kind of white that led one to believe the guy had a weakness for whitening treatments.

The guy had to know a lot about makeup and skincare, because his skin was flawless. He looked young, but seemed to be very well dressed for a college student, and very . . . manicured. I certainly hadn't been that well put-together when I was attending the Royal Academy. He seemed too put-together even for a makeup artist—he looked more like an actor dressing up for an audition.

"What were you two looking at?" I asked, pointing at the tablet in her hand with a tip of my chin.

"Oh, nothing," Sam replied dismissively. "I was just showing Fern some of our makeup techniques."

"Should I go and come back another time?" Fern asked, turning to Sam.

"I think that would be okay," Sam replied with a certain uneasiness.

Fern said goodbye and was about to walk past me.

"Wait, shouldn't he stay and watch you do touchups?"

"Right!" she replied, her eyes widening as if she was coming out of a daze. "Of course you should stay, Fern. What was I thinking? Come stand behind me and you can watch me work."

"Can I take notes?" Fern asked, and his question seemed to surprise Sam.

"Yes!" she replied, smiling brightly. "Yes, of course you can. Hugh, please sit down. So, Fern, I don't know how familiar you are with the type of schedule we have here on set, but the first thing I have to do is make sure I keep a certain consistency with the actor's makeup, especially between scenes. Years ago they used to take pictures and keep them in the makeup trailer, but nowadays we can rely on different types of visual aids. All the makeup artists have tablets available with how the makeup for each actor should look. You might know this from school, already, but I do have to admit, sometimes I use my cell phone on a day-to-day basis, as it is more practical to have when we're shooting outdoors."

As she started reapplying the makeup, Sam proceeded to explain the details of her work process, and Fern kept watch studiously while taking notes. Of course, I could only watch for so long since she was touching up my makeup and I had to keep my eyes closed.

At some point, maybe lulled by the sound of her voice, I must have fallen asleep. I felt a hand gently shaking my shoulder and a feather-like kiss on my cheek.

"Hugh, wake up. Honey, they need you back on set . . . come on, wake up."

"Hmmm . . . what's going on?"

"You fell asleep while I was giving a makeup lesson . . . *so rude*. You know, my area of work is not that boring, Mr. MacLeod."

The tone of her voice was stern. I peeked through my heavy eyelids, thinking she'd smile and admit she was joking. Instead, she shook her head, her features tensed with annoyance.

"Mmhmm," I said, stretching my arms above my head, trying to wake up. "No, you're right, it isn't. I didn't fall asleep because I was bored, I can tell you that much."

"Then why did you?"

I yawned and she gave me another sour look.

"I'm tired, okay? Still trying to get back in the swing of things. You know how hard it is to get used to these twelve-hour workdays all over again. Plus, *neach gaoil*, it was your voice that made me fall asleep."

"My voice! My voice is responsible for making you fall asleep? You embarrassed me in front of Fern!"

"Who?" I asked, scratching my head, racking my brain

for answers.

"Fern, the intern."

"Ahhh! The intern. Dinna worry, Samhain, I'm sure he doesn't mind."

"Of course he doesn't, but I do! Can you try not to fall asleep next time? You were snoring. It was embarrassing."

I pressed my eyes shut, still trying to wake up from the involuntary nap that had put me in a comatose state.

"Okay, okay. I promise I won't do it again. Now, what am I supposed to do next? Do they need me back on set?"

Her harsh glare told me I wasn't back in her good graces yet, but I knew it wouldn't be much longer before I'd make my Sam smile again, because that was what we did. I grabbed her left hand and brought it to my mouth, kissing her knuckles, running a finger along the sensitive skin of her wrist. She squirmed under my touch and laughed. I smiled at her, and when she realized it had been a ploy to get her to be nice to me, she shook her head and narrowed her eyes.

She let out a huff and playfully grabbed my chin in her hand then leaned down and gave me a small peck.

"What am I going to do with you, Hugh MacLeod?"

"Forgive me for falling asleep?"

"Maybe, but when we get home, first you worship me like a queen, and then you go straight to bed, understood? No sports channel for you tonight."

I nodded and gave her a tight-lipped smile. I was trying to get her to crack out of her serious mood, but her eyes remained unaffected—not even the smolder could win her over. Maybe it was time for new weapons of seduction, and

A Scottish Wedding

I had a few in mind.

What I didn't expect when we got home was to find the entire place upside down.

SAM

"What's all this?" Hugh asked as he surveyed the new furniture.

"Well, we were going to be at work, so I told Gordon to let them in." Gordon was the previous owner of the cottage. He lived in St. Martin and used to rent the cottage out, but he wasn't social media savvy—his words—so he hardly had any customers these days. Plus, at seventy-seven, the upkeep had become too much for him.

Ever since Hugh bought the place, he'd given him work to do. He'd been surveying the work on the cottage when he was away, and according to Hugh, he'd keep an eye on things whenever we weren't in Scotland.

"Let who in?" he asked.

"The delivery guys."

"Did you buy the entire store?"

"Ha ha. I was tired of sitting my ass on that old sofa we got from Gordon. It was a nice gesture, but that's one of the most uncomfortable couches I've ever sat on. Luckily IKEA offers delivery and installation. You should be thankful I didn't ask you to do it. I had Rob put together all my furniture back in LA—in exchange for money, obviously."

During the last few weeks, we hadn't had that much time to shop for furniture. We had ordered an expensive bed online and paid a hefty fee for expedited delivery. I had gotten a few things for the kitchen, including a small table and chairs, and Hugh had made the time to order a big flat-screen TV and have it installed—*of course.*

But, we hadn't gotten any living room furniture yet, since we rarely had time to browse and decide on something. So, I just went online and added to the cart whatever we needed. My ass was begging for mercy—I could only stand to sit on the worn-out floral couch from the 60s for about fifteen minutes at a time.

The furniture was scattered all over the place, not arranged with any kind of logic.

They had probably left it that way since they had no idea how I wanted it, but still.

Men.

"Babe, help me move this couch over here," I asked him.

He lifted the couch on his end and I did the same on mine, and we placed it in front of the fireplace.

"Why didn't you try to get something different?"

"Different? You mean something that isn't mass-produced?"

He gave a slight shrug.

"Well, anything else would have taken weeks, if not months, so ease of access and availability of product, for one, and ease of delivery and assembly, for two. Plus, it's durable and affordable. Honestly, I see no point in buying expensive furniture, especially with kids." I grabbed some throw pillows and arranged them on the couch.

Hugh was in the kitchen, grabbing a drink, and I heard the thud of something falling to the floor.

I glanced at him, his eyebrows pulled in a frown, his

mouth slightly ajar. He was staring at me and didn't seem concerned about retrieving whatever he'd dropped.

"What was that? Did you break something?" I asked, not understanding what his confused look was due to and why he kept staring at me.

"Sam," he said in a low voice. "Is there something you need to tell me?"

"About what? The furniture? Yeah, I like it. I'm sorry if you don't approve. I think it's functional."

"Do you realize what you just said?"

"That it's mass-produced but well done and functional? What did I say?"

"Are we having kids now? Is there anything I should know?"

Oh. Oh. Oh.

I felt my cheeks redden—scratch that, felt my face *flare up*.

"Oh, that. That came out, huh? Those words came out of my mouth," I said, half to myself.

He nodded, walking my way and closing the distance between us. The look in his eyes was a mix of marvel and confusion.

"So, you were saying . . . there's no point having expensive furniture with kids around?" he asked.

I shook my head. "There isn't. It's a waste of money. Better to have something cheap and replaceable for the first few years," I said, almost in a daze. His expression was serious and solemn, but his blue eyes sparkled and hypnotized me. He let out a deep breath through his nose and then wrapped his arms around me.

"So, kids?" He gave me a small grin and my body

relaxed in his embrace.

"Yeah, kids. Someday?"

He wrapped his arms tighter around me.

"Yeah, someday . . . someday soon?" he asked, his accent more pronounced.

"Soon-ish?" I replied with a tentative smile.

A bright smile stretched across his face, and it made his eyes look even more beautiful. Actually, his entire face looked gorgeous. He looked . . . radiant.

If happiness had a face, it would look the way he did right then. He was *beaming*.

"Soon-ish sounds good, but let's not wait too long. I don't want to be an old dad."

"Ha! You're only thirty-four."

"Yeah, but my dad already had three kids at my age. I don't want to pressure or rush you, but I'm looking forward to it, *neach gaoil*, verra much."

He ran his fingers through my hair and placed a kiss on my lips. Then, he asked me if I needed help with the other pieces I'd ordered.

That night, we arranged the furniture in our very first home and laid the base for our life together. It was going to take time, but I couldn't wait for the day we'd be ready for the next step. Before that, we'd have to get married.

Hopefully I would hear back from our attorney—soon.

Chapter 9

SAM

Our cottage nestled in the beautiful valley on the coast of St. Martin was the perfect place to relax and unwind—too bad it always felt like we were constantly on the go with very little time to kick back. In the evening, my heart would ache to go back home, and it didn't have anything to do with the fact that I was tired. I had a serious case of longing for my little house. I wanted to stay there forever. The place was simply magical.

Of course, it might have been because I had the best roommate one could ask for, and maybe also due to the fact that trying to be professional at work was increasingly difficult. At the end of the day, I ached to go back home with my man, but it wasn't just that. There was something about seeing the cottage in the valley and the sea on the horizon that relaxed me instantly. Sometimes we'd leave before dawn and I couldn't see a thing, could only hear the lulling sound of the ocean waves in the distance.

Coming home in the evening was also one of my favorite things.

Home sweet home, indeed.

Most times, we'd eat what craft services had prepared, but a few days a week, I used my brand-new crockpot—I had given Cecilia the one I'd purchased last year.

"I made a stew for this evening. Did you have dinner already?" I asked Hugh once we took our jackets off.

He exhaled a deep breath, and his eyebrows pulled together in a frown.

"Not sure I can eat that, *mo chridhe*."

"It's okay if you're not hungry. I can put it in the fridge and reheat it tomorrow."

"It's not that . . ." He hesitated, looked down for a second, and when his eyes met mine again, there was a look of weariness mixed with . . . *embarrassment?*

"I can't eat your stew, Sam, or pretty much anything you cook, unless it's allowed by the plan."

The plan?

I narrowed my eyes. "What plan?"

Another deep exhale. What was stressing him so much?

"Winston said I got too soft around my middle. He's putting me on a low-carb diet."

"What?"

"He said I got a little fat, and he's not wrong. I did gain some weight, just a bit," he said, patting his stomach. "I gained over half a stone in the last few months. I have been working out, but I haven't been so good at keeping track of my diet. I need to get back on track." He ran a hand down the back of his head, messing up his hair, making it look completely disheveled. There was a hint of shyness in his eyes, as if he needed to apologize for something.

I was so confused.

My man had to be on a diet? I mean, I knew he watched his weight and what he ate, but he worked out a lot, and we had long days. He didn't seem to have this issue. Then again, we hadn't lived together, so I didn't really know how strict his diet had been in the past. Before, it seemed he was following a high protein but well-balanced diet.

Now his trainer said he was fat?

"Bullcrap," I muttered in disbelief.

"It's true," he replied, his accent coloring the words with a different sound than what I was used to.

"Wait, what's a whole stone? How many pounds is that?"

After a short Google search, we established that a stone was fourteen pounds, and Hugh had gained over half a stone, which meant he'd probably gained about eight or nine pounds at the most.

"I just want you to know you are perfect to me, just the way you are. How dare Winston say you look fat?"

He gave me a shy smile followed by a nod.

"Well, he said I got soft in the middle."

"Soft?" I asked in a horrified tone.

"That's what he said."

"I don't like Winston Styles very much anymore. How could he? How could he tell you you're going *soft*?"

"It's not that big of a deal, Sam. I just have to do it. I

don't have much of a choice, after all."

"No one can tell the difference, Hugh, believe me. I touch you all the time. You are anything but soft."

"I did gain weight, Sam. Don't say I didn't. Look." He took off his thermal Henley and stared at me with arms open to show me I was wrong. Well, maybe he was just slightly, *slightly* less taut around his waist, but I would call it slight bloating, not weight gain.

"This is insanity," I muttered. "And if you're soft, what does that make me?"

Granted, I wasn't the one who often had to be shirtless in front of a camera. Still, I instinctively looked down at my belly and tightened the muscles of my abdomen, trying to make my little pouch disappear, and Hugh noticed.

"Don't. Don't do that, Sam. You're beautiful. I love this spot right here," he said, brushing the skin right below my belly button, "this slight curve here . . . that leads to the sweetest valley." His accent was maddeningly sexy when he spoke in a low, gruff voice.

I loved the way he said *valley*. It drove me insane, just like his touch.

His fingers across my belly sent a shiver traveling across my skin, and a sweet ache bloomed between my thighs.

"And I love this," he said, tracing the curve of my hip, going up to the hollow of my waist, tracing a finger around the curve of my breast.

I sighed and looked up to him. His eyes were the bluest of blue when he stared at me intently, with arousal, but then something flashed across them, as if he'd forgotten something, and the maddening intensity disappeared.

A Scottish Wedding

"Winston just wants to make sure I get back on track and keep up with the regimen I was following. He said it might be difficult with my fiancée spoiling me at home. I'll have to be strong and resist your culinary talent, lass."

I shook my head as I kept surveying the area. *Soft*. What an absurd notion.

"Well, I haven't been here long enough to do much damage. Winston should really blame it on the press tour."

"He does. Oh well, whatever—all those croissants in Paris were *worth it*," Hugh said with a grin and a dreamy look in his eyes. He then let out a sigh and my chest filled with a strange ache. *This happens to Hollywood actresses all the time*, I thought. My sister followed an elaborate plan constructed by a nutritionist, but luckily, she never had to starve herself. It was my first time witnessing this type of situation, and I was a bit sad for him, I had to admit.

I knew when it came to his career, he would do almost anything. I threw my hands up in the air, resigned. He needed to do what he needed to do.

"Okay, so what can I do to help? Do you have a meal plan?"

As it turned out, Winston had Hugh signed up for one of those fancy meal delivery plans Hollywood stars are known to use. Surprisingly, they delivered the food all the way up to St. Martin, and the very next day, we had a huge delivery at the set. All of Hugh's food for the entire week was carefully labeled and placed in a giant cooler for us to take home.

"Mornin', Sam," Winston said with a cheery smile as I exited Hugh's trailer. I knew he was there for a midday workout session with my beau. The right word to describe Winston was imposing, with his above-average height and solid frame. With his carefully styled dirty blond uppercut, short beard, and piercing blue eyes, he had that mix of charm and roughness that women seemed to like so much. I knew I was right because I had seen pretty much every straight woman on set swoon for him as much as they did for the male lead and other hunky actors on the show.

"Don't try to charm me, Winston. You're on my shit list."

"Aye, lass, go easy on me, will you?" He let out a guffawed laugh, and I glared at him.

"Seriously, Styles, if you're not nice to my man, I will cut you. How dare you tell him he's gone soft?"

"It was just for motivation. He has some important scenes coming up, and he has to look his best. He agreed with me."

"Pfff."

"Don't be mad at me. I'm just doing my job. Besides, don't you want him to look hot?"

"He already does," I replied, folding my arms across my chest. He gave me a sardonic smile and I let out a frustrated breath. "Look, I get it, it's your job to make him look his best on screen. Just . . . go easy on him, okay? I don't want him to get stressed out about his *nonexistent* gut."

He nodded slightly, bidding me goodbye. "You have my word . . . sort of. I'll *try* to go easy on him."

A Scottish Wedding

I shook my head and walked back to the makeup trailer.

HUGH

A few days later, we were about to head home for the day when a buzzing sound coming from Sam's mobile distracted her. She turned around to grab it, and as she read her notifications, I saw her eyes cloud over. She sat down on the chair behind her, still reading the message on her phone.

"Sam, what's wrong?"

"My sister is missing. No one knows where she is." I saw the look of terror wash over her features, the color disappearing from her face. "How is that possible?" she asked herself.

"What do you mean, Sam? What happened? What's going on? Where is Amira?"

SAM

"No one knows," I replied in a choked voice. "Not my parents or my brother. Not even her publicist knows where she is. My mother told me something happened. Some pictures . . . oh my God, what has she done?"

I logged back into the laptop and searched for the latest info on Amira Farouk.

"Oh, fuck. Didn't she realize someone was taking

pictures of her? How fucked up was she? Look!" I told Hugh, urging him to look at the pictures that were now apparently all over the Internet.

"I really don't want to see pictures of your sister naked, if that's what you're looking at."

I almost snorted before I realized that whoever had done this might have even more explicit shots of her. I shook my head and pressed my lips together. "It's not that. This is what happened," I said, turning the laptop around so he could see.

The pictures were of Amira and another girl kissing, and not just small, chaste kisses. It was an intense make-out session with tongue and touching—a lot of touching. Thankfully, she wasn't naked in the photos, but I didn't know how much difference that would make. As a popular actress, my sister had an image to protect. In the last few years, she'd become the press's darling, and despite Hollywood still being quite racist at heart, Amira had found a good amount of success as an actress of mixed heritage, one whose skin and looks were not like those of America's other sweethearts.

She had been able to get ahead thanks to her skills and good looks, on top of her easygoing personality. I was afraid something like this would damage her reputation forever.

Sure, times had changed, and a scandal in this day and age wasn't always a bad thing—celebrities seemed to bounce back from public upsets like nobody's business. Nude pictures, tone-deaf comments, anti-Semitic remarks, sex-abuse allegations . . . the public opinion these days seemed to get past the most obnoxious things and shoved them under a rug—or was that accurate only when it came to rich

A Scottish Wedding

and powerful white men?

My brain kept rambling on its own as I clicked on every shady blog that had posted the pictures of my sister's "Sexy Night Out." I simply couldn't help myself, in a way. I needed to see the extent of the damage with my own eyes.

Poor Amira.

I was a bit puzzled by the pictures I was looking at, because my sister had always been cautious as to whom she hung out with. She knew she needed to surround herself with a few trusted friends, and I was positive none of her friends had done this. I didn't recognize the girl she was kissing; she didn't look like anyone I knew.

My mind kept rambling, so much so that I'd managed to shut Hugh out, who had apparently been trying to get my attention.

"Do you know who she is?"

"No. I have no idea how this could have happened—I mean, unless the phone of the person taking pictures was hacked. I don't recognize the other girl. The people in Mira's circle would never betray her trust like this, and now no one can get ahold of her? My mom said she's not at her house in LA or the one in New York. None of her friends have seen her since the pictures leaked. Where could have she gone?"

"Did your sister always swing both ways?" he asked in a low, tentative tone.

"No, I don't think she's bisexual, at least she never gave me that vibe. I never . . . we never talked about it." I hesitated, trying to recall any situation that might have been an indication of Mira's preferences.

He cocked one eyebrow and gave me a slight shrug.

"I mean, she very well could be. Maybe she's just now trying to figure it out herself."

Hugh wasn't wrong. *Have I been missing the obvious?*

"You don't think she was just having fun? Kissing a girl out of curiosity?"

"Maybe, or maybe there might be more to it, and it might be the reason no one can get ahold of her. Maybe she's not ready to confront her feelings and face her family. She'll turn up somewhere. Your sister is not stupid. At the moment, she's probably just deeply hurt and confused. Hopefully she'll get in touch with someone soon."

Chapter 10

SAM

I couldn't really sleep when we got home that night. I kept trying to send text messages to Mira and she never read them. I wondered if she even had her phone with her. I wondered if she'd left it behind, trying to ignore the mayhem happening online. Mira's publicist and attorney seemed to work around the clock to get all the websites to take the photos down, and by the time I had to go to work again, I could hardly find any links. But, the articles were there, as well as the ones speculating about Amira Farouk's sexuality.

Hugh had tried to distract me, talking about the script for the upcoming episode and asking if I would rehearse some of the lines with him, but I couldn't stop thinking about my sister.

It was nighttime in LA by the time we woke up and got ready to go to work.

I texted my mother asking for news, but she said she hadn't heard a thing. She was pondering the possibility of filing a missing person report if Mira didn't show up within the next day. For some reason, my mother was deciding to rely on her hippie "skills." She said she had a strong feeling that Mira was okay, and it was just a matter of time before she would turn up to one of us. I didn't understand why my mother felt so confident about that, because on the other hand, I kept thinking something might have happened, especially if the people she was hanging out with were people we didn't know.

"What does Daddy want to do?" I asked my mother over the phone.

"Oh, you know your dad. He thinks we should have already filed a report. He doesn't want to wait." Not a whole lot of people knew this, but unlike what's repeated over and over in crime shows, you really don't have to wait a twenty-four-hour period before you can file a missing person report with the police.

"Mom, what are we going to do if she doesn't answer our calls and messages? Are we going to keep waiting? I think Dad is right—if we can't locate her by tomorrow, you should go to the police."

"Fine, honey. I will think about it, but you know, my chakras are telling me everything will be fine in just a few more hours."

I rolled my eyes at the word *chakras*. "Fine, Mom. Whatever you say."

"Love you, honey. Give a hug to my future son-in-law.

A Scottish Wedding

Don't worry too much about your sister. Her skin is just as thick as yours."

I sighed, hoping my mother was right.

By midday, I had almost made myself sick with worry. I was so preoccupied with thoughts of my sister, I didn't eat and hardly had anything to drink. I started feeling lightheaded and grabbed a bottle of water from the fridge in our trailer. On my downtime between scenes, I sent a couple of emails, messaged Fern, and tried Amira's phone again.

Everyone around me in the makeup trailer kept chatting away, but my mind was elsewhere. I was glad no one had asked me about Mira, because it meant people hadn't seen any headlines with my sister's name. Our days were so busy and we were so removed from the rest of the world, most of the time it was rather easy to remain oblivious to what was happening out there. Or maybe they had seen the headlines and didn't ask about it to be nice.

By midafternoon, I was going crazy. My mother hadn't heard from her yet, and I was starting to fear something really bad had happened to my baby sister.

Nothing my sweet Hugh said or did could distract me.

Then, a production assistant came in the trailer looking for me. He said someone had asked for me outside but they didn't have security clearance, a man who very much looked like a driver. Tall and sharply dressed, he looked like he could be in his late forties, according to the assistant. He said it was important, that I should go right outside.

"American or . . . ?"

"Scottish, by the looks of it."

"Hmm, I wonder who it is." I was mid-touchups on Hugh, so I was a bit reluctant to follow him right away. A small spark of hope ignited in my chest, and after exchanging a look with Hugh, I knew I had to leave everything and go.

"Cecilia, can you take over for me? I need to run out a moment." Then, I leaned down to kiss Hugh's cheek. "I love you. I hope it's who we think it is. I'll be back as soon as possible."

I walked outside with my heart hammering in my chest, hoping my instincts were right.

God, I hope it's her.

I opened the car door hastily, and when I looked at the person in the back seat, I took a deep breath.

"Amira Rose Farouk, what the hell are you doing here?"

"Hey, big sis," she said with a wave of her hand. "Nice seeing you too."

"Yes, I think . . . I think there's more to it. It wasn't just a one-night transgression just for the fun of it."

"Amira, what are you trying to say? Are you gay? Bi? Confused?"

"Confused sounds about right."

In her darkest hour, Amira had reached out to Declan, asking him to fly her out as close as possible to St. Martin. She had met him in London, and he'd flown her out to Edinburgh through the private jet company he worked for.

I had never asked Amira about her fling with Declan in the past, because I didn't want to meddle in something she wasn't ready to talk about, but given the circumstances, I had to ask her. When I inquired about Declan, she said she liked him all right, but they'd decided months ago to remain friends, for several reasons.

Distance was one of them. The fact that Declan had two little kids that required stability was another. In the end, they decided they'd be better off as friends.

I exhaled a deep breath, feeling a bit relieved. I had no idea what had happened between them after their hookup in Thailand and I felt reassured by the fact that Amira had called him in a moment of need. Clearly, they were on good terms.

But now, I had a different set of revelations to deal with. I scooted closer to her on the couch and smoothed her hair behind her ear.

"Have you always felt this way?" I asked in a soft tone.

"I'm not sure. I've always been so focused on my career. Guys were around, and you know that growing up I didn't care much for them . . . but then something changed. I started noticing them, but lately . . . I don't know. I've noticed how no one piques my interest at all, and I haven't been in a relationship in a while. Even when I was dating that young producer, I wasn't that into him. The sex was . . . just okay. I don't know, Sam. I kind of got into a funk, and

I started thinking maybe I don't like guys that much in general."

"Maybe you just had a lousy lover. Since then you've had other sexual encounters, right? Did no one rock your world?"

"Yes and no. I always felt . . . detached, in a way. Not present, not in the moment. Not completely connected or satisfied. And in the meantime, I've started noticing other things . . . about women. The way they look, the way they feel. I wanted . . . I wanted to explore that. I wanted to see how I'd feel . . . with a girl."

"And? Has it happened yet?"

"Yes. A while back."

"And it was a more . . . satisfactory experience?"

She gave me a shy nod. "It was."

"Was it mind-blowing?"

"You could say that."

"So . . . you and this woman are . . . in touch? Were together and didn't work out?"

She looked away. "We are in touch, but it's complicated. Her schedule is as busy as mine and we don't live close. And now . . . this mess."

I sighed. "So, you like girls. Big deal."

"See, that's the problem—I don't know. I'm not a hundred percent convinced. I *think* I still like guys. I feel attracted to them. It doesn't always happen, but sometimes it does."

"So, you're bisexual."

"Maybe. I guess. God, I don't even know," she said, covering her face with her hands.

"I get that the pictures were not the greatest way to

announce it to the world . . . but, if you're bisexual, what's the big deal? Are you worried about your career?"

"No . . . yes. Yes, of course I'm worried about it. Are you so wrapped up in idyllic Scotland that you forgot how ruthless Hollywood is?"

I narrowed my eyes at her.

"No, I haven't forgotten, but I think maybe you're exaggerating. I know it looks bad now, but when things calm down, no one is going to care who you fuck in the privacy of your own home."

"You're wrong. Everyone is going to care, and I'm going to stop getting roles. I will no longer be the darling Amira, and the press is probably going to murder me. Gahhh, I can't even think about what they're going to try to pull in interviews." She let out a sigh and then rested her head on the couch, staring at the ceiling.

"Mira, come on, take a deep breath." I took one of her hands in mine. "I think you're losing perspective. There are quite a few bisexual actresses in Hollywood and they're doing just fine."

"Oh yeah?"

"Yeah. Have you forgotten about Anna Paquin? Or Evan Rachel Wood? I don't think their careers have been suffering since they came out as bi. It's true, you had a certain image until now, but you're growing up. You got into this business so young, and you were so focused on your career . . . how could you even have had the time to figure out what you want, what you like? If this is who you are, don't try to repress it. Just be yourself."

"Sam, you make it sounds so easy."

"You're right, it's not easy, and it probably never will

be, but if you try to repress your true nature, you will only end up living a terrible life, filled with regrets. You'll never be at peace. I want you to be happy, sis."

She gave me a soft look, and for the first time I saw a hint of a smile brighten her face. Her eyes, though, still looked melancholic. She curled up around me and placed her head on my shoulder, sighing again. I reached around her with my arm and caressed her back.

"This is going to kill Daddy," she uttered.

I snorted. "Ha! Don't think so highly of yourself. If Mom divorcing him and then coming out didn't kill Dad, he'll be fine. He might be shocked, and he'll worry about you, but he's a parent—he'll always worry about you, and he'll always worry about me, even though I'm doing fine. Same goes for Rob—though maybe Dad actually should worry about him. I have no idea why it's taking so long for him to become the next Evan Spiegel."

I snorted a laugh, and she started laughing too.

Our little brother Robert was one of the few handsome techy guys of Silicon Valley.

The problem was, he still hadn't made it big. For the last couple of years, it had seemed he was on the verge of success, but it hadn't come yet.

I knew he was working on a few different apps, but I didn't know enough to understand the dynamics of the business.

"You'll see, Mira, everything will be all right. Things may look bad now, but it won't last. In the meantime, you're welcome to stay here as long as you want."

"Thank you, though I do hate to impose. It doesn't feel right to crash your love nest."

A Scottish Wedding

"Don't worry about it. Hugh has four brothers, I'm sure he understands," I said, patting her head gently.

I took off the rest of the day to take care of her, and even though I knew she needed me, I felt a pang of guilt for leaving the set and everything else behind. I was sure Nora wasn't too thrilled about me leaving for the day, but I couldn't leave Amira by herself. As soon as we'd gotten to the cottage, we'd informed our parents she was with me. She had a good cry with Mom on the phone, and after she hung up, she had a good cry on my shoulder. It had taken a while for her to open up, and we were finally touching the surface of the problem.

My chest tightened at the thought of my sister receiving any kind of backlash, and my heart ached thinking that for months, if not years, she'd been confused and hadn't been able to open up to me, her sister and one of her best friends.

We sat on the couch, hugging and staring at the kindling flames in the fireplace.

A while later, I heard a car outside, and I knew Hugh was back.

When I got up and opened the door, I was surprised to find he wasn't alone.

His costar Melissa was with him. *What the what?*

"Hey Sam. How's Amira?" she asked, but when she caught sight of my sister on the couch, she dodged me, heading for the living room. Amira, who had fallen asleep on my shoulder, was rubbing her eyes.

"Mel!" Amira said. *Mel?*

They stared at each other for a few seconds before embracing in a tight hug.

I could hear Melissa's muffled, "I am so sorry, I am so sorry," and I was so confused.

Amira and Melissa had met a few weeks ago when we were in Japan to promote the show. We'd had dinner together a couple of times since Amira had flown in for business herself, and we'd spent a day going around Tokyo. At some point during the day, though, we'd parted ways. Hugh and I had decided to go to Ueno Park and the National Museum of Art while they wanted to go to Shinjuku to check out a bar Amira had heard of.

Hugh and I stared at the two of them wrapped in a tight embrace in the middle of the living room. We frowned at each other, confused as to what was going on.

Melissa disentangled herself from Amira and took a step back to look at her. She brushed away a strand of her hair, caressed her face, and then took her hand.

She leaned in and whispered something to my sister.

A smile broke out on Amira's face—the first I had seen since she'd arrived. She took Melissa's hand and led her to her room.

"Well, that's an interesting turn of events," my fiancé said.

I turned around to look at him. He was laughing, but I, on the other hand, was even more confused.

"You can say that again . . . do you actually have any idea what the fuck is going on?"

"I guess in due time, they will let us know," he replied, snickering.

Chapter 11

SAM

A few days later, we were informed by my mother that things were calming down.

Amira's publicist had been working relentlessly on getting the compromising pictures removed, and by some kind of miracle, there was a new scandal everyone was more interested in: some "it" couple from a popular show was calling it quits, and now all eyes were on them.

She didn't seem to want to leave, and I wanted her to stay for as long as she needed to. Hugh wasn't complaining about it, either.

"She's your sister, Sam. She needs you right now. It's not like I haven't had to watch over my brothers before," he said with a sad grin.

"Who? Ewan?" I asked. He was silent for a moment, his

eyes drifting away, and replied with a solemn nod. Ewan MacLeod was the troublemaker of the family. According to Hugh's mother Fiona, the youngest of her sons had a certain penchant for trouble. Like his namesake Ewan McGregor, the youngest MacLeod had a weakness for motorcycles—a weakness his mother wasn't too fond of—but that was the least of the MacLeods' problems when it came to the baby of the family.

"When Ewan was in high school, he got mixed up with some real bad people, ye see . . . he'd managed to make friends with the worst group of young blokes in Oxford, of all places. Small theft, drug use, you name it. It's a miracle he was never caught, never arrested." He caressed my face, his eyebrows pulled together, his eyes clouded by the memories. "Of course, that's nothing like what your sister is going through right now, but with Ewan, it seemed that none of us could really get through him. There were a few months when we didn't know how bad things were. He was despondent, hardly attending school, fighting with my parents constantly. I was already out of the house, so I didn't live all of it firsthand, but one day, I found him outside my building, in Edinburgh. The look on his face . . . it's something I will never forget," he said with a low chuckle.

"Here he was, this young arrogant brat who refused to listen to his parents and obviously had been up to no good for who knows how long . . . but he'd come to me, at last, and he looked *broken*. He had gotten into a fight with someone, that was easy enough to tell. He had a swollen, bruised eye, face covered in bloody marks he'd tried to clean best he could, but his eyes . . . they reminded me of when

A Scottish Wedding

he'd fall off his bike or wouldn't get his way as a child. When we got upstairs, he told me what happened. He'd finally realized what we'd been telling him all along about these kids he'd been hanging out with. He'd seen their true colors, the ones of young criminals. There was more they were doing besides selling a little weed and coke, and Ewan didn't like what he'd seen. He had tried to get out, and they let him, but not without beating him to a pulp. He was too proud to go back home and Declan had a family already, so he came to me. So, my point is, Amira came to you because she knows she can count on you, and I don't care how long she stays. She's family. My family is yours, and yours is mine," he said, placing a soft kiss on my lips. His words and his warm breath eased the tension I'd felt ever since Amira showed up.

He broke the kiss and glanced down at me, as if to make sure his words had had the desired effect. I stared into his deep blue eyes, placed my hands on his strong shoulders, balanced myself on my tiptoes, and kissed him again, slow and deep.

Once again, he reminded me of how deep my love for him was, how deep it ran into my bones.

Passionate, brave, and steady, he seemed to have a gift for making me feel grounded when life threw curveballs that had me spinning. I was reminded that he was absolutely the one for me, the only one I wanted to build a family with.

He was the one who'd started making plans for our future, but it was now my turn to show him how much I wanted to be tied to him for the rest of my life.

Till death do us part.

My plan simply had to work.

The next Saturday, we were taking a walk on the beach. The weather had been great during the week, but we had to be at work. Now it was cloudy and a bit chilly, but it wasn't raining, so we decided to get out and about. I asked Amira about Melissa. It didn't make any sense to me why they were so close, but Amira told me they'd had a "moment" together when we were in Japan and had been in touch ever since. I'd known about Melissa for a while; she'd told me she was gay the previous year when the network was pressuring her and Hugh to pretend to be involved to create more hype about the show.

Even after Amira's explanation, I was still shocked that the two of them had clicked so fast.

"Melissa is so sweet," she explained. "We've been messaging and talking a lot in the last few weeks. She's been trying to help me. She's so gorgeous, and so down to earth, too," she said, almost sounding star-struck herself.

I was glad my sister had someone to talk to, but I still felt a bit sad that she hadn't tried to open up to me sooner.

"Wow, now I kind of get it," she said wistfully.

"What?"

"I get why you weren't the same when you got back to LA. This place . . . it's like it gets under your skin. It makes you yearn for it, even if it isn't your home."

"I know. The longing . . ." I knew what Amira was

talking about. When I had gotten back to LA, I had a terrible case of Scotland sickness. I missed it so much, more than I ever thought possible.

"It's so . . . peaceful here." She let out a deep breath, but when I looked at her, her eyes were dull, as if someone had sucked the life out of my spunky sister. I couldn't stand it. I had always felt protective of her and it hadn't changed growing up. Even now, I wished I could shelter her from all the pain, public shaming, and heartbreak. She was just a young girl like many others, having fun with friends, but now those pictures were going to come up in random conversations and interviews for who knew how long. The curiosity surrounding public figures was sometimes sickening. It seemed like people forgot that even actors and celebrities had feelings and were riddled with insecurities just like everyone else.

"If I were you, I would never want to leave," she joked, and this time there was a dim spark in her eyes.

I took her hand and gave it a squeeze.

"Come on, let's reach Hugh. He's already up on the hill," she said with a smile.

"I told you it was hard to keep up with him."

"Race you up there!" Amira said in a tone as mischievous as the one she'd used when we were kids.

"Come on, not fair!"

Chapter 12

SAM

"What exactly am I doing here? Sitting on your couch, moping, interrupting your blissful premarital cohabitation?"

I patted her on the leg. "You're just taking a break, Mira, and you came to your big sister because you know you can count on me . . . and because I kind of live on the edge of the world, or it feels like that sometimes. Plus, wasn't I the one moping on your couch last year? You almost made it to your thirties without a scandal—give yourself a break."

"I forgot what a great movie this is." She sighed, pointing at the screen. We were watching *10 Things I Hate About You*. We'd watched it so many times growing up, and it was definitely a favorite of ours.

"It really is. I'm kind of sad we both missed the

A Scottish Wedding

Shakespeare craze of the late nineties. I was talking to Dad about it once, and I swear he named at least twenty different movies that were made between 1990 and the year 2000 that were based on or inspired by Shakespeare plays."

"Gahhh, I would love to be cast in a Shakespeare adaptation. I've been dreaming about it forever. I have been actually thinking about doing a play, but I haven't heard of any interesting projects."

"Well, I'm not sure if anyone is doing Shakespeare movie adaptations these days, but if they did, why wouldn't they cast you?"

"I don't know, I can just see the casting director telling me I'm 'not a good fit.' I'm neither a Viola or a Juliet or a Katherine."

I shook my head. "I think you're overreacting. You're definitely not a Juliet, but I can totally see you as a Katherine. If you want to do a Shakespeare adaptation, do a Shakespeare adaptation. If they won't let you, do it yourself."

"What do you mean, do it myself?"

"Write it."

"Like Mom?"

"Sure, why not? And, I mean . . . write it, produce it, direct it. If there's something you want to do, start now. It doesn't matter when you get there. If it's something you're passionate about, it won't matter if it takes a year or seven. Rome wasn't built in a day and all that."

She nodded thoughtfully, as if seriously considering the option. I wasn't sure if my sister really wanted to take on more responsibilities behind the camera, but I would go for anything that would distract her from her momentary drama.

"Good Lord, Heath Ledger and Julia Stiles are just fabulous in this movie, aren't they?" she asked.

"They really are. There's something so easy and natural between them. You know what? Watching this movie makes me realize something else."

"What?" she asked with a curious look in her eyes.

"This might sound stupid coming from a makeup artist, but I kind of miss the days when you could still see flaws on an actor's face. Look, you can see their blemishes and little skin imperfections, and their teeth are not all veneers. They have real, authentic smiles. They look more . . . human."

"Are you saying your job makes actors look inhuman?" she joked.

"I'm just saying the makeup and lighting and cosmetic adjustments actors go through these days make them too *perfect*. This idea that you have to be *flawless* is kind of twisted, to be honest, and the stress of striving for perfection makes people insane, if you ask me."

She took a deep breath. "You're not wrong. It's not like I haven't done the same over the years. It's so easy to obsess over, and now that you're pointing it out, I'm kind of upset these actors get to look so normal in this movie and we can't anymore."

Amira ended up staying a few more days, and each day

A Scottish Wedding

her mood seemed to get progressively better. I still had to go to work, so I didn't get to see her until the evening. She was enjoying spending some time alone, away from the madness, or so she said.

Her publicist and her team had successfully gotten the pictures removed from the Internet, and as often happened with these kind of scandals, the finger was pointed at the hacker, not the starlet. I was relieved, and I hoped in a few months she'd be able to feel less wounded about the whole ordeal.

On Friday night, a week after she arrived, we took her to the pub. If people knew she was in town, they had been quiet about it, for which I was thankful. I'd told only a handful of people I worked with that my sister was there, mainly the makeup crew.

I knew they wanted to meet her, but they understood she wasn't much in the mood for company.

When we went out that night, Amira arranged her long blond locks in a braid and wore a black baseball hat. She dressed casually, covered head to toe in black, and borrowed one of my heavy-duty rain coats. Apparently, she was having just as much of a hard time adjusting to the weather as I had. Sometimes I still struggled with it, but I was lucky I had my hot-blooded Scot to warm me up whenever I needed it.

When we stepped into the pub, karaoke night was already in full swing.

One of the cameramen was singing a feisty version of Blur's "Boys and Girls" and had the whole place singing along and dancing. I had seen this place get rowdy before, but this was stadium level. People were going gaga, dancing and singing at the top of their lungs. It was only about eight thirty in the evening, but it was evident the drinking had been going on for a while. I laughed to myself and shook my head. The people I worked with were quite the party animals.

My sister's eyes were wide with wonder and excitement and the smile on her face was one I hadn't seen in days. I smiled back at her and led her through the crowd to find a more secluded spot by the wall. She squeezed my hand as we made our way, turning her head around, taking everything in, looking at every little knickknack hanging on the walls of the pub. Hugh was right behind us, acting a bit like a protective big brother and personal bodyguard. The expression on his face was not relaxed as usual, and he kept looking around as if trying to spot anyone suspicious whom we might have to steer clear of.

He leaned in and brought his lips to my ear. "Are you two going to be okay if I go get drinks?"

"I believe we'll manage, dear sir," I teased him, giving his hard bicep a squeeze. He rolled his eyes, but I still managed to steal a kiss.

"I'll see if I can find Cecilia and send her over."

"Great thinking," I replied.

I watched Hugh make his way through the crowd, heading for the opposite end of the pub, where the bar was. I glanced around us, just to make sure we weren't attracting too much attention. Besides a few quick appreciative glances from locals, I didn't think anyone had recognized my sister yet, which was what I wanted. I just wanted Mira to have a night of fun—incognito, if possible.

After "Boys and Girls" ended, Rupert took the stage.

A Scottish Wedding

"Well, this is new," I said, mostly to myself. "I have never seen him karaoke the whole time I have been here," I explained to Mira.

As soon as the notes of "Mr. Brightside" by The Killers filled the place, the crowd went insane. If I thought they were being wild before, it was nothing compared to this.

You would have thought this was everyone's all-time favorite song.

Almost every person in the pub was singing and jumping.

It was exhilarating.

Excited by the crowd's reaction, my sister joined in and pulled my hand so I would start jumping with her. It wasn't hard to convince me to go with it.

We sang and danced along with the crowd, and everyone was so loud, I couldn't even hear Rupert. I got a glimpse of Hugh trapped on the other side, waiting for things to calm down before he made his way back to us.

When the song was over, everyone settled down a bit, and it wasn't long before Hugh was back with us again and then Cecilia, Oliver, my fellow makeup artist Blair and Mika joined us soon after.

We chatted as we could between songs, and even as I snuggled against my Scot, I tried to keep a watchful eye on my sister and everyone present.

When we'd go out in LA, it was normal for her to get recognized everywhere she went. It didn't bother her, and sometimes she got a good laugh when people approached her even when they thought she was a completely different actress or got her name right but the name of her latest movie wrong. With the upheaval of emotions she'd been through in the last few days, I just wanted her to be able to relax and be herself, without having to have conversations with complete strangers who would most likely be asking for selfies.

After song after song, however, she seemed to grow restless. She was still dancing along to the music and following the conversation, but she was a bit . . . off.

"I'm going to the restroom," she said, leaning down and giving my hand a squeeze.

"Do you want me to come with you?"

"Nahh, I'll be fine," she replied with a confident smile.

I let her go, because I hated being the overbearing big sister, and Amira was a grown-up who could take care of herself. While she was gone, I was challenged by Blair to a round of tequila shots, and the sting of the alcohol helped eased the tension I had been feeling since we'd gotten there. I just needed to relax. No one was going to recognize or bother Amira. Everything was well. I had nothing to worry about.

By the time Amira came back to the table, she had a bright smile on her face and an extra skip in her step.

"Are you okay? You look chipper . . . like, a lot chipper."

"You're right, I am. I feel fantastic, like I'm finally getting back to being myself again. You know what?"

"What?"

"Fuck the haters and the naysayers. My life is my life. I do what I want. I call the shots."

I pursed my lips together, trying to hide a smile, but inside, I was simply ecstatic.

This was the Amira I knew.

She was finally going back to her old self.

"And you know what I realized?" she asked.

I shook my head no.

"What better way to celebrate my newfound empowerment than to sing with my sister?"

"No, Amira. You didn't!" Now it all made sense: she had put in a request for karaoke.

This wasn't what I wanted. I didn't want to attract attention to us, *to her*.

"I did, and you're going to like it. Besides, it's going to bring the whole pub *down*."

"Oh yeah? And what is it we'll be singing?"

"One of our favorite karaoke songs . . . *ever*. We must have sung it a million times as kids."

"Argh, you didn't!" I knew exactly which song she'd picked. "It's 'Wannabe' by the Spice Girls, isn't it?" I asked. She grinned obnoxiously, and her good humor was infectious—I couldn't say no. I didn't know how to say no to my little sister.

"Oh man, you will *pay* for making me sing *zigazig ah* in front of all my coworkers."

Along with all the other oldie-but-goodie songs of the night, "Wannabe" was a hit.

Did I stumble a few times on the lyrics? You bet. That song is impossibly fast, and we hadn't "performed" it since we were in middle school or something, when the fascination with karaoke really started weaning out.

Just like when we were kids, she sang Scary and Baby Spice's lines while I sang Ginger and Sporty's. Don't ask about Posh, because as we learned by watching the video a million times, she didn't have any solo lines in that song. In retrospect, Posh seriously banked by being in one of the most successful girl bands ever. *And*, not only had she married one of the most swoon-worthy soccer players, her Victoria Beckham dresses were amazing. I had seen a couple in Mira's closet and they were constructed beautifully.

A few people recognized Mira after our performance, but she was in a far better mood by then so she didn't really hate saying hi or posing for a couple of pictures.

By Sunday evening, Mira had a flight booked and her luggage packed.

Gone was the somber look in her eyes of a few days before.

She was back to her old self, ready to take the world by the balls.

"You were right, Sam. I just needed a break. I needed time to put things into perspective. This wasn't as bad as it could have been. So there's a picture of me going to town with a girl out there—big deal. My life is my life and I don't have to explain myself to anyone."

"Atta girl!"

"You know, I think this place is magical." She let out a small laugh, eyes brimming with a mix of mischief and excitement. "I feel completely . . . *rejuvenated*. Now I know where I need to come any time I feel down."

"You're most welcome to come visit any time you want. In fact, I might need you to be back in just a few weeks," I explained, letting her in on my plan.

Chapter 13

HUGH

After Amira left, I thought Sam and I would have more chances to spend some time together.

Unfortunately, it wasn't like that.

My trainer had not only cut a consistent amount of calories from my diet, he had also increased the frequency of my training sessions and now insisted on me training during the weekend, as well. The last thing I wanted to do after a long week was get up early and leave my Sam alone in bed. I would have much rather buried myself in her than have to get out and work my arse off at the gym.

I wanted to take another walk in the heather just like we had a couple of weeks before, but we never had a chance.

On top of everything else, when I asked her about wedding plans, she always sounded evasive, although she did say she had talked to the attorney and we were close to obtaining the necessary paperwork for a license.

We'd gone to Edinburgh on a Saturday to sign the deed for the cottage. The lawyer, Damon, was an old friend of mine from when my family used to live in town, and he didn't make too much of a big deal about having to meet us during the weekend. That being said, I could tell he was recovering from a long, drunken night by the disheveled way he looked when we met up with him.

After we signed the papers, he invited us to go out with him, and I was half embarrassed when I had to explain I was on a new regimen and couldn't go out and drink. He assured Sam and me that he would take care of the paperwork for the marriage license, but we hadn't heard anything back yet. I considered giving him a call, but when I mentioned it to Sam, she assured me she'd been in touch with him and there was nothing new to report. "Besides," she'd said, "since we won't have time to get married until next summer, it won't matter whether we can have a license now or not because they're only valid for a few weeks."

We had completed the first month of shooting and wrapped the first two episodes of season two. The next few months were going to be even more challenging because of what was going to happen with Abarath's storyline. My diet and the training were weighing on me, and I didn't have time to make plans with Sam about our wedding.

I realized how cranky I sounded, when I really shouldn't have.

True, I was having to make some sacrifices, but I was also living my dream, and every night I shared a bed with the woman I loved.

A Scottish Wedding

Still, it was hard to always have a positive attitude. There were days when exhaustion could easily turn me into a grumpy jerk. To make things worse, Sam seemed to spend way too much time with Fern the intern.

It seemed I could hardly get a moment alone with Sam on the set—Fern was *always* around.

Whenever I'd look her way or go to the makeup trailer, the two of them would always be engrossed in a hushed conversation about . . . something, sometimes giggling, laughing together like old friends. When I'd ask what it was about, Sam would always reply with some makeup lingo and procedures I didn't know anything about.

I couldn't help it—I was suspicious. The guy was good-looking and sharply dressed, and for some ridiculous reason was always buzzing around my beautiful fiancée.

I shouldn't have been jealous. I should have been trusting.

I knew Sam would never betray me, knew she wasn't the type of person to do that.

But I couldn't help it.

"Why is Fern always around?" I finally asked her one Friday evening while we were on our way to the pub. Fern came two to three times a week and stayed for a few hours, but he would only work with Sam. He followed her wherever she went, meaning he followed her on set and even watched when she did touchups.

"Who?" she asked with an air of confusion.

"Fern. Why is he always around? Why is he always working with you? Why can't he work with someone else?" I snapped.

Sam let out a laugh. "You're kidding!"

"I'm really not. I'm dead serious. I can't even have a conversation with you anymore because the bloody bloke is always around!" I said, the tone of my voice going involuntarily higher. It seemed I couldn't control it.

"Hugh, he only comes twice a week, three at the most. You have plenty of time to talk to me during the other days. Besides, this is not something I decided. The network wanted to do this, and I think it's a great opportunity for Scottish students. Don't be so *daft*!"

"I've seen the way he looks at you!" I yelled, despite my better judgment.

"You can't be serious," she said in a low voice, disappointment clouding her features.

"Don't tell me I'm wrong. I've been keeping an eye on him. He fancies you!"

"You're ridiculous. I'm pretty sure Fern is gay—not that I've asked him, because it's none of my business—but honestly? I'm disappointed in you. Do you really think I would cheat on you? With him? Under your nose?"

"Don't tell me it's not possible, Sam. Didn't the same thing happen to you? Wasn't your boyfriend cheating right under your nose?"

She shot me an angry look. "I can't believe you just said that to me. How could you? Do you really think I would ever do anything like that to you?"

Shite. I was fucking everything up.

"No, no," I replied. "I didn't mean it like that. It's not that I don't trust you . . . I don't trust *him*."

"But if you do trust me, there shouldn't be any problems whatsoever. I love you, and I would never do something like that to you. If you don't know that by now, if you don't trust me enough to know nothing is going to happen, I don't know what the point of getting married is."

The harshness of her words cut like a knife. No, this wasn't what I wanted. I knew I was overreacting, but it was as if I were spiraling and couldn't stop.

"No, Sam, I trust you."

"Do you? Because that doesn't sound like it at all."

"*Mo chridhe*, I'm sorry. I love you. I didn't mean to hurt you."

"Yeah, but you did. Those were harsh words MacLeod."

I tried to take her hand as we continued toward the pub, but she pushed mine away.

"I'm sorry," I said again, even though I knew it wasn't going to fix things, not right away, anyway.

She stopped in her tracks before we approached the door of the pub.

"You know, one of these days you'll realize how terribly wrong you are and you will feel so stupid—seriously, *so* stupid—and you know what? I can't wait for you to admit how wrong you were."

I already felt like an arse, knew I had royally screwed up, so I didn't say anything. I simply nodded and gave her a cautious look.

"You're right. Can I hold your hand now?" I asked tentatively.

She stared at me with narrowed eyes. "No, you can't."

She entered the pub, waved to our friends, and headed to the bar without waiting for me. From a distance, I saw her order and down a drink before going over to Philip, the guy in charge of karaoke.

Mika saw me and came over to say hi. He patted me on

the back.

"What's up, man?"

"Not much. Making an arse of myself, mostly."

Mika noticed me watching Sam, and probably saw her shoot me an angry look from the other side of the pub.

"Fuck, man. What did you do?"

"Not what I did, more what I said. Should have kept my bloody mouth shut."

"Come on, let's have a drink."

"All right, just one though—Winston will have a cow if I get drunk and get off his strict regimen."

We ordered whisky at the bar, and while I sipped, I felt everyone's eyes on me. Sam and I rarely had a row, so I knew everyone could tell something was off. Then when I turned around and saw that Sam had taken the stage, things only got worse.

"This is for you, Hugh MacLeod," she said, but something in her tone was off. Her voice was cold and distant.

This wasn't going to be good.

When I recognized the song—"Borderline" by Madonna—I felt everyone's eyes on me even more. I got so uncomfortable, I almost wanted to jet out of the place. She wasn't going to let me down easy. Admittedly, I deserved it.

She sang the entire song while staring at me, looking proud and focused.

At some point, I raised my glass to her and took a drink of whisky.

I was hoping my gesture would make her smile, but it didn't work. She narrowed her eyes at me even more.

I wanted her to forgive me, but I wasn't going to

humiliate myself. If this kind of "shaming" was the sort of punishment she had in mind, I was gladly going to put up with it.

Everyone cheered when the song was over, and for a moment I thought I'd have to chase her out of the pub and apologize profusely. Instead, she surprised me again.

She walked toward me and stopped a few inches away. I stepped forward and placed my hands around her waist then leaned down and kissed her forehead slowly, tentatively.

"I'm really sorry for what I said, Sam," I whispered in her ear.

"If you ever act like a jealous grouch again, I swear I'll knee you in the balls," she threatened.

Ouch.

"You have my word," I told her, and then I sealed my promise with a kiss.

Later that night, it was all forgotten. It was almost as if nothing had happened.

By the grace of God, Sam was sweet and loving as ever. She might have been furious a couple of hours before, but any trace of bitterness was gone. I couldn't deny how relieved I was.

While I couldn't drink much, everyone around me kept drinking merrily, including Sam, and I had to admit I was a wee bit jealous. Winston's program was taking a toll on me.

Drinking out together was our way to unwind after a long week, and it wasn't very much fun to make one drink last while everyone else kept downing their glasses. Mika and Frank in particular had one too many, and were trying to get me to join them on a bike ride the next day.

"You two will be too hungover! You're not going to be able to bike down the hill to save yer life!"

Mika raised one eyebrow. "Want to make things interesting? I bet you twenty quids I'll go faster than you, uphill or downhill. You down for it?"

"Sure, why not. Twenty quids." We clinked glasses and I took another—small—sip of my whisky. I glanced to my side and found Sam, Cecilia, Blair, and the newest addition of the crew, Gretchen, engaged in a heated conversation.

"All I'm saying is that I don't think anyone has ever spoken the words 'Oh my gosh, I am so sick of this song.' That song is a freaking *classic*. You could make me listen to it a hundred times in a row and I wouldn't be sick of it. I've been listening to it since I was a teen, and it still gives me chills." Sam was arguing with Cecilia about something.

"Oh, bloody hell, don't tempt me. You know I love a challenge." Cecilia bumped her shoulder against Sam, and then clinked her glass with the one my girl was holding.

"Ha! Do you?" Sam replied in a mocking tone. They narrowed their eyes at each other and scrunched their noses playfully, as they often did. Cecilia was a constant tease, and Sam was a good sport, most of the time. The interactions between them were like those of two sisters. In fact, Sam and Cecilia's relationship was quite similar to the one she had with Amira. I was happy Sam had someone here in Scotland whom she was close to. It couldn't be easy to be away from her family all the time. I knew she missed them terribly, even if things were easier this year. We had each other and I didn't doubt for a moment that this was where she wanted to be, but sometimes I felt a little pang of guilt.

I knew I missed my family, and I was just a few hours away from them so Sam and I could visit whenever we wanted. She was close to her mom and dad, as well as her sister and her brother. Even if she didn't admit it, I knew that from time to time, she probably missed the chaotic, sunny LA life.

I got distracted by the guys talking about rugby and chimed in to comment about the latest match, but then I drifted back to Sam and Cecilia's conversation. I took another swig of my whisky and zoned in on their chat, but I still couldn't quite understand what they were discussing since I'd missed the beginning of it.

"What are you two talking about?"

They both turned in my direction, surprised by my interruption.

"Your girlfriend—pardon me, your *fiancée* here claims that 'Everlong' by the Foo Fighters is the greatest love song ever. I mean, it's not a bad song, but the *greatest*?"

I let out a low chuckle, and Sam didn't miss a beat to make her argument.

"Well, it is *my* favorite love song, Cecilia, it doesn't have to be yours. I'm not expecting you to feel the same way about it. We can agree to disagree . . . wouldn't be the first time," Sam told her before raising her eyebrows and continuing. "I know it's unusual, but it's a song I have listened to a million times and I could never get sick of it. It's sweet and sexy and it has that *I'm falling for you and if we do this right it could be the greatest thing ever* vibe. Does that make sense? And, it's not cheesy. For the life of me, I *cannot stand* cheesy love songs," she said animatedly. She was clearly a bit intoxicated, and for some reason I found it really amusing when she was slightly drunk.

We locked eyes, and a slight smile stretched across her face. Whatever she was thinking about made her blush ever so lightly. She chewed on her bottom lip and then brought her eyes down to her glass.

Cecilia huffed, eyes widening in exasperation, her cheeks colored a faint pink.

"Fair enough. I can agree with your point. What's your favorite love song, Hugh?" Cecilia asked, and the question made me freeze for a moment. I couldn't think of one.

I hadn't ever been in love with anyone before Sam.

"I don't suppose I have one in particular . . . though I have to admit, 'Brown Eyed Girl' will always have a special place in my heart." I winked at Sam, biting my bottom lip, and she smiled, memories brightening her gorgeous, dark chocolate eyes.

Then I thought about the song Sam had been talking about.

Everlong. I'd always liked the song, though I couldn't say I had paid much attention to it in the past. Sure, it was a great one. I revisited the lyrics of the song in my head, and somewhere along the line, I found myself agreeing with my bride-to-be. Indeed, it was a great song, and now that I knew how much Sam loved it,

A Scottish Wedding

I couldn't stop thinking about it. Several scenarios popped in my head, and at last I had an idea I hoped I could make come true at some point.

SAM

"Cut!" someone called, and everyone started shuffling around set again.

These naked scenes were draining, and not just for the actors. There were too many crew members all packed in a very small place, and it was always warmer than usual because the actors were butt naked and everyone was sweating profusely.

In other words, the most unromantic setting ever.

But, it had to be done. The scene in question was pivotal, and was basically changing the course of the characters' lives.

Abarath's only true love, Leonia, had escaped from the castle once she learned he was in grave danger. Dressed as a boy, in true Shakespeare fashion, she'd managed to recruit a few people to help her out along the way, and had been able to rescue Abarath, who was being held hostage by some roamers who learned he might be in possession of a magical dragon tooth, one that had healing powers.

The legend of the healing tooth was an ancient one, and Abarath didn't have much to do with it, but he'd drunkenly claimed he had such a thing in his possession. A few days later, word reached Leonia's kingdom that Abarath had been captured.

Leonia shed her damsel-in-distress clothes and went

after the man she loved. Now that she had found him and the two of them were away from the castle, she wasn't ready to let go of him.

It wasn't very princessy of her to give up her virginity to a man she could never marry, but she was determined to seduce Abarath, if necessary.

I couldn't fault her.

The man was hot. Abarath was strong, brave, and charming . . . and so damn good-looking, he even made a modesty patch look sexy.

If I were a princess and couldn't marry the man of my dreams for some stupid dynastic reason, I would feel the same way.

I was really surprised by the evolution of her character in the last couple of episodes, and I had to give it up to Melissa for nailing every nuance of Leonia's personality. She was a really great actress.

I walked over to Hugh just as an assistant was handing him a robe. *Pity.*

But, all in all, it was better this way. Sure, I could be professional, but let's face it: it was so hard to focus when my man was naked right in front of me. The year before, I'd had to try my hardest to hide every bit of attraction I felt for him, but now that we were together, it was possibly even tougher to hide the way he could stir up my insides with just one of his looks.

He put on the robe as his eyes met mine. He winked.

What a tease.

"Stop looking at me like that," I told him with a pointed look.

"Looking at you like what?" he asked innocently.

"Like you're not the one naked, wearing a tiny modesty patch."

His eyes sparkled with amusement and the corner of his mouth tilted up.

"*Mo chridhe*, I'm wearing a robe," he teased.

"Yeah, but you're naked under it, and you've been naked this entire time . . . and you've been doing . . . *things*."

"Things?" The entertained tone in his voice was hard to miss.

"Yes, things, things that make my mind . . . wander."

"Ahhhh." He nodded in agreement. "So, the *things* I was doing made you start thinking about other *things* . . ."

"That's right."

"Is that why you had your head stuck in your tablet?"

I let out a breath. *Lie.* "Yes. You were seriously killing it, but all of a sudden I felt pretty caught up in it . . . and I had to look away. My mind went elsewhere and I got carried away. It was . . . too much."

He ran his thumb across my cheek while I patted his face with a sponge to reduce the shine on his forehead. He looked down, smiling wickedly at me. Oh, him and his bedroom eyes—I wanted to kill him sometimes. I couldn't stand when he tried to get me all worked up in public, and I hated to admit how easy it was.

"Stop it, I said! I'm trying to work here," I mumbled, frustrated, blood rushing to my cheeks.

"Fine, I'll behave—for now," he teased in that low and rumbly accent of his. It sent a chill down my spine. Oh, how I loved the sound of his voice.

I sighed, partly from relief and partly with frustration.

"But before we go home, you should stop by my

trailer," he suggested with a wicked grin, eyes beaming with mischief.

I couldn't hold back my smile. "A trip down memory lane? Sign me up."

Chapter 14

SAM

"How many times did I tell you not to bring your toys home, Hugh MacLeod?"

He laughed, impenitent, and marched into the living room carrying two ancient-looking swords. Of course, I was familiar with them, had seen swords like those before—they were the props he used on set during fight scenes.

They weren't dangerous, but they had been made as heavy as real swords to make the fight scenes more realistic. As a result, wielding one of those fuckers could give you some severe arm and shoulder pain if used the wrong way.

"What are you doing with those things? You're not supposed to steal from the set, you know that. I might have to report you," I teased.

"Uh-huh, you do that," he replied, unfazed. He walked

to where I was sitting on the couch—relaxing, mind you—and handed me one of the swords.

"What am I supposed to do with this?"

"Humor me, Sam."

I gave him a quizzical look. "I don't think I understand. Do you have a scene to rehearse? I don't think I'm the best person for it."

"You're the best person for everything."

"Well, love, I can't say I'm not flattered, but you're mistaken."

"I disagree." He started moving the furniture in the living room. First the coffee table, then the two armchairs, and when he still wasn't satisfied with the space he'd cleared, he pushed the couch back while I was still sitting on it.

I narrowed my eyes at him, and he leaned down and kissed me on the lips.

I didn't reciprocate the kiss, so naturally he kissed me again and again until I gave in to whatever charade this was.

"I was reading, you know," I grumbled.

"And I need your help. I need to rehearse this scene and someone distracted me last night and made me forget I had lines to learn." He winked at me, and I blushed, thinking about the night before. Yes, I might have been guilty of keeping him up too late.

I laughed and shook my head.

"You didn't seem opposed to my plans last night."

"How could I have been?" he replied with a wicked, teasing look. "But I do have lots of lines to learn, and I need your help. So, be a good sport and help me out, aye?"

He handed me the sword again—I had refused to grasp

it before—and I discovered this one wasn't as heavy as I remembered.

"Uh, this one isn't as heavy as the one you normally use," I said as I swung the sword around, feeling the weight of it.

"That's because we have different ones depending on the actor's build. I'm surprised you don't know this already, Ms. Hollywood," he teased.

"Har har! I've never worked on a historical or fantasy drama before," I reminded him.

"True," he agreed. "Up you go. Come on, Sam. Help me out. Besides, didn't you tell me you took fencing for a while?" He smiled and stretched a hand toward me, and I finally got up.

"I knew I should have never told you that! I took fencing when I was fourteen! Besides, the weight of the fencing bow can hardly be compared to this thing!" I'd told Hugh the story of when, inspired by a summer of watching Valentina Vezzali's accomplishments in the fencing disciplines during the 2000 Summer Olympics in Sydney, I had decided to take up the sport. I regretted telling him that now.

I was fourteen when I took up fencing, and although I was truly enthusiastic about it for a year, I had become self-conscious as my body started changing and I became curvier. I felt exposed in the white fencing uniform, especially against the rest of my teammates, who were mostly slender California blondes, and I gradually talked myself out of it.

I loved the sport, but I honestly believed I got started too late.

"Okay, so what do you need me to do?"

He handed me a script and told me whose lines he needed me to read.

In this scene, Abarath was facing off with an old frenemy who had been trying to undermine his reputation across the kingdoms.

For the next hour, I read and fed him lines when needed. I jumped on the couch and tried to fight him with all my strength. We dueled, we laughed, and minute by minute, I enjoyed it more and more. I loved the life we were making together.

We were two souls from very different backgrounds, but ultimately, we loved the same things, and loved our jobs so much, even when it was hard, even on the days it reduced us to grumbling, tired shadows of ourselves.

I got caught up in my thoughts and soon he disarmed me, a wicked grin plastered on his face as I knelt down to retrieve my sword.

"You're going off script!" I protested after taking a better look at the lines just as he managed to pin me down to the floor.

He pointed the fake sword to my neck, albeit gently. He towered over me, breathing heavily, a mischievous look brightening his eyes.

"Now that you're my prisoner..." he started.

"Again, off script," I mumbled, looking at the stage directions once more.

"Shhhh, Sassenach. Now that I disarmed you, you'll tell me everything I want to know."

I frowned. "Meaning? If this is about Fern again, might I remind you I'm in the perfect position to kick you in the groin."

He huffed. "Nah, this isn't about Fern. This is about you and me."

"I don't understand," I replied.

HUGH

"I know you've been keeping secrets from me. Fine, I was wrong, verra wrong about Fern, but you . . . you have been hiding something. I can feel it, Sam," I told her, still catching my breath.

"You're wrong."

"Am I?"

"Yes," she replied with a certainty that made me suddenly question my motives, but I had to know. She'd been evasive for *weeks*. "If there's anything I'm hiding from you, it's stuff that you don't need to know to begin with."

"Like what?"

"Like my wedding dress, you moron!" she yelled.

My face fell, and it took me a few seconds before I could say anything.

"I didn't know you'd been looking." It was all I could muster.

"Of course I have! These things take time, and in case you forgot, we kind of work and live in a place at the edge of society, where things are not exactly accessible."

I nodded. She was right . . . but there were other questions that came to mind.

"So, you've been dress shopping, but what about setting a date? And what about the attorney and the paperwork? Any time I ask you about it, you change the subject."

"Can I get up yet? Or do we have to keep having this conversation with me at your mercy?" She shot me an angry look.

"Of course. I'm sorry." I gave her a hand and pulled her up.

"Was this whole scene just a ploy to ask me questions? Could you not just ask me what you needed to know?" Her eyes searched mine, looking worried.

I let out a nervous breath. "Yes . . . no. I really did need your help rehearsing the scene, but I did have a few things to ask, and it feels like we never have time to talk about our plans. I know we want the same things, but I keep worrying that after we wrap season two I will have to travel to promote the show and we won't be able to make it happen, and I want to. It's so . . . strange, Sam. It's strange to want something so badly when just a while ago you didn't even know if you wanted it to begin with. Ye ken what I mean?"

She studied me for a moment, and then a smile stretched across her face, reaching her eyes, illuminating her pretty face.

"I ken," she replied, mimicking my accent.

I dropped the prop sword on the floor and took her in my arms. She wrapped her hands around my neck, but when I tried to lean down and kiss her, she pulled back.

"There's more you want to know, isn't there?" she asked.

"Yes, there is, but now I feel like too much of a dafty to ask any more questions."

"Just ask me whatever you want to know," she

reassured me. "If there are things we haven't talked about, it's because I know how much stress you've been under. I noticed you haven't been your usual self, especially since Winston made changes to your training schedule. Hugh, the last thing I want is you doubting me. You should always, always be able to tell me what you think and ask me what you want to know."

"Okay then, what's going on with our paperwork to get a license? What have you heard?"

She smiled big. "It's almost ready. The attorney said it was all just a matter of clarifying my immigrant status here. He seems to think it might be just another week or two and then we can apply for a license, which would be great if we actually had the time to get married right now." Her eyes widened, as if she finally remembered something. "What else? Is there anything else you want to know?"

"Have I not scared you off with my mood swings? Do ye still want to marry me?" I joked, looking at her sheepishly.

She breathed a laugh. "Yes, I still want you, mood swings and all, but I will do anything to corrupt the screenwriters and convince them to give your character a belly next season. Seriously—this thing where you almost have to starve yourself is unacceptable."

"I'm not starving myself. The only thing I'm always starved for is you."

She shook her head in disbelief. "Don't you try to butter me up. I can see it in your eyes. You look tired, worn out. I understand Abarath is going through some shit this season, but I really don't want to have you go all method. It's not healthy for your body, either."

"Since we're talking about wedding plans, is there anything you want to mention?"

"Well," she started. "I have been contacting venues around here. You mentioned a church in Stonehaven, and I have been trying to get in touch with a priest and find a nearby place where we can have the reception, but it all depends. I can't give them a date until we know the show's plans for next summer. I don't know when they will fly you out, when you're going to have time off . . . so it's all up in the air. Besides, people around here take wedding plans *seriously.* Some venues are booked up two years in advance."

"Two years? I had no clue."

"I know. We might have to get married in a barn, if it comes down to it," she said in a low tone, almost as if she were talking to herself.

"A barn, a pub, a movie set—I'd marry you anywhere," I told her, tracing the profile of her nose with my own. I searched for her mouth, and she responded to my kiss, keeping her lips pressed against mine for a few seconds.

"Good to know. Looks like we'll need to be flexible."

"Forgive me for being a stubborn arse?"

She laughed, and the beautiful noise filled the room. I cherished the sound of it. I loved her laugh, the way her face lit up, the way she looked at me, the way she could be patient with me even when I didn't deserve it.

"I forgive you for being a stupid arse. Besides, I don't think you can help yourself. It's a natural trait."

I frowned. She might have been right, but I was taken aback by her words.

"What do you mean?"

A Scottish Wedding

"Your mother seems to think stubbornness runs deep in the MacLeod blood. She told me I better get used to it."

I laughed softly, and she smiled at me.

"Hold fast?" I asked her once more.

"Hold fast," she replied. She looked at me, eyes full of love and understanding. On her face was the kind of sweet smile that had made me fall for her, the kind I wanted to see for the rest of my life.

Chapter 15

SAM

I entered his trailer in one swift move, like a ninja.

It was crucial that no one saw me—Lord knows what people would say if they saw me in the *wrong* trailer.

He turned around in his chair and by the way his eyebrows shot up, almost reaching his hairline, I'd say he looked just as surprised as I thought he would.

"Sam, what are you doing here? Is Blair okay? Is she sick?" Mika asked.

Blair?

Oh, right. Blair was the makeup artist working with him. My colleague.

He frowned at my silence, his eyes filling with worry.

So, are they "on" again?

Never mind, I didn't have time for that.

A Scottish Wedding

I shook my head. "No, no. Blair is fine. She's around . . . somewhere. I'm here to talk to you."

His expression relaxed instantly, but then he frowned again, taking in my words.

Mika and I were friendly, but we were definitely not friends. He and Hugh and the guys used to hang out a lot . . . whenever Hugh and I weren't holed up somewhere together. He was always hanging out with the guys when we were in a group, and I never had a chance to work with him one-on-one on set, so I didn't really know him that well.

What I did know was that I needed him to be my ally. I hoped he'd join my team without asking too many questions, and hopefully keep his lips zipped about the truth.

"Mika, I need your help."

"What's going on, Sam?"

"I need you to do something for me."

He shrugged, his lips curled into a small pout. "Sure. Anything you need."

"I need you to take Hugh away for the weekend."

A small laugh escaped his lips and as he grinned, his dimples made an appearance.

"Take Hugh away? Are you already trying to get rid of him, Sam? Is the honeymoon already over?"

I chuckled. *It hasn't even started*, I thought to myself.

"No, silly, but there's something . . . I need to have the weekend to myself. It's . . . important, and I can't tell you what it is, but I promise it will be worth all your trouble . . . once you find out what it is."

His frown deepened and he looked even more

confused. I wasn't making any sense, and I was aware of it, but I couldn't explain any further.

"So, you can't tell me what it is . . . but can you at least tell me what you expect me to do? What is it exactly that you want from me?"

I exhaled a deep breath. Of course, I had been rambling so bad, I hadn't even explained what I needed him to do.

"I need you to convince Hugh to go to Glasgow with you. There's this CrossFit convention and this guy Hugh has been following is going to be there. He loves his videos and tutorials. He's been talking about him practically non-stop," I said with a slight eye roll. "I guarantee you he'll jump at the opportunity as soon as you mention it."

"Who's the guy? Do I know this dude?" he asked.

"Probably. His name is Boyd Rivers. He's American, but he lives in Amsterdam. He has a gym chain in New York or something like that?"

"The name does sound familiar," Mika replied pensively.

"Anyway, you have no idea the trouble I had to go through to get these VIP passes. They were sold out, and I ended up calling the guy and explained my situation to him and his wife—who's a really cool chick, by the way." Mika's blank expression told me I was rambling again and not making much sense. I took a deep breath and tried to put my thoughts in order. "I know I'm confusing you. Bottom line: I need you to take Hugh to this fitness convention in Glasgow and make it look like it's your idea. That's all you need to know."

He closed his eyes and shook his head. He pursed his lips and let out a deep breath through his nose. He was

A Scottish Wedding

going to say no.

"I don't know, Sam. I don't feel good lying to Hugh. Why can't you just give him the tickets yourself? As a present?"

"Because he'll figure out I'm trying to get rid of him for the weekend."

"Well, aren't you?" he mumbled.

"I am, but . . . it's not what you think, I swear. I just need some time away, and I can't get away without . . . ruining everything." I let the words out and stared at Mika's suspicious face. This wasn't going like I'd planned. I felt my heart sink into my stomach, and without even realizing it, I sort of dropped to my knees in a rather dramatic fashion. It hadn't been my intention to beg, but if seeing me drop to my knees was going to seal the deal, so be it.

"Mika, you must know how much I love Hugh, and I'd never, ever do something to hurt him. I'm trying to do the opposite. I want to make him happy for the rest of my life, but I need just a couple days without him to make that happen. When you find out why, you'll be glad you helped. That's all I can say."

"Fine," he replied in a low grumble.

Elation coursed through my body, and I felt immediately lighter.

I jumped up to my feet.

"Thank you! Oh, thank you, Mika! You won't regret it, I promise." I gave him a kiss on the cheek, and he almost pulled back in surprise. Just then, Blair entered the trailer.

"Hey, I was looking for you. It's time to come to the makeup trailer, Mr. Hollywood," she said in a mocking tone.

I turned around and a slow, sly smile stretched on her face as she noticed me there. "Were you telling him about this weekend?" she asked me.

I nodded.

"Wait a minute, *she* knows?" he asked, sounding outraged. "You told Blair but you won't tell me? Why can you tell her but not me?"

"Because she's part of my plan, and with you playing for the other team—AKA my fiancé—you're most likely to betray my trust."

"I'm an actor, Sam! I know how to keep a secret!" he let out, frustrated, raising his hands up in the air rather dramatically.

"Do you? Is that why everyone in town knows about your crush on Blair? Is it because you know how to keep a secret?"

My words hit home, and he lowered his eyes after briefly glancing at Blair.

"That's between me and Blair," he said sheepishly.

"Shite, Sam. Did you really have to bring that out?" Blair said. *Yikes*. Maybe I had said too much. All this planning was messing with my head; I was so focused on the goal, I was paying no attention to the lines I was crossing.

I let out a breath and ran my hands through my hair in frustration.

"I'm sorry," I said to them both. "I really am. I didn't mean to meddle in your business, but if I can give you a small piece of advice, from someone who's been where you guys are right now, it would be that you have to talk to each other. Stop playing games. Stop lying to yourself," I said, locking eyes with Blair. These two had had their ups and downs since last year. Apparently, they'd been hot and cold for months, and no one knew about it until Mika spilled the beans on a drunken night out.

Still, I couldn't risk it. My plan was all I had. When I thought about it, when I pictured it all in my head, I couldn't wait to see how Hugh would react.

I had kept secrets before, had lied before, when I was trying to get my revenge on Eric, but it was agonizing to keep things from Hugh. I couldn't wait for him to know *everything*. My plan simply had to work.

"Mika, back to us," I told him, locking eyes with him. "Here are the VIP passes, and I will email you all the info with your accommodations. I'm counting on you. Don't let me down—you're my only hope," I added with a pleading smile.

He ran his fingers across his jaw, twiddling with the scruff on his face.

"Fine. You have my word. I won't say anything. Whatever you're planning, it better be good," he said with a pointed finger.

"Yay!" I jumped up and down on the spot and he laughed, his features suddenly relaxed and more beautiful. I looked at him, but he'd locked eyes with Blair, who was standing right behind me. The laughter subsided and it was replaced by an intense look that made me suddenly feel like a third wheel.

"Okay, thank you. I'm leaving now. You won't regret it, Mika," I told him, and he brought his attention back to me, giving me a nod of his head. I headed for the door.

"You two better be good to each other," I said without turning around, loud enough for them to hear me. "I'm watching you."

HUGH

"What's this?"

"Um, I don't know. A box?"

"I can see that, but what's in it? Is it more merchandise for the show?"

"Maybe." Sam smiled, being awfully coy. She opened the lid and pulled something out. "Tadaaa!" she exclaimed, holding the item in the palm of her hand.

"What's this? A *candle*? With my face on it?"

She grinned, her eyes twinkling, her face beaming with far too much excitement. I frowned. I didn't know how to feel about this. T-shirts were one thing, but candles?

Really?

"What does Abarath smell like?" I read out loud, noticing the tagline on the candle. "What do I smell like?" I asked with a frown.

"Uh-uh, not you, *Abarath*," she corrected.

"What does he smell like? Sweat, dirt . . . grass, and on occasion, foul dragon blood, if I had to guess."

"Pfff! You're no fun. Don't you dare kill the dream, Hugh MacLeod. You gotta play the game now that you're a sex symbol."

"Am I?" I said with a confused chuckle.

A Scottish Wedding

"Yes, of course you are. Where have you been the last few months? People love the show!"

"Oh, really? They do?" I was teasing her mercilessly.

"Okay, stop making fun of me, funny guy," she said with a half-smile. She opened one of the candles and took a whiff. "Hmmm, these smell good . . . kind of like . . . citrus and wood? Here," she said, handing it to me. "Your fictional alter ego smells really good."

"M-My fictional alter ego smells good? Is that supposed to be a jab?" I joked.

"Don't get butt hurt. That's not what I said," she replied innocently, but the expression on her face was anything but. "So, how was that CrossFit convention you and Mika went to?"

"Oh, trying to change the subject, are ye?" I teased her, and she slapped me on the arm.

"I am not! I just want to know how it was. Did you guys have a good time? You got home so late last night, I didn't have a chance to ask you." That was true. We didn't have time to talk about how our weekend apart had been because after a testosterone-fueled weekend with my costar, the only thing I wanted to do when I got back home was give my lady a good ride. I'd missed her. Besides, Mika was too much of a bletherer. I liked the bloke in small amounts, but a whole weekend with him was far too much.

"I'm afraid the production is wasting their money—no one is going to buy those candles."

"Agree to disagree," she said, taking another whiff of the candle. She placed it down on the counter and I turned it around, not wanting to stare at my own face. She glanced at her phone.

"We're running late—I have to get you ready before Nora gets on my case. So, the convention? Was it worth it?" she asked.

"It was incredible. I wish you could have been there," I said, and she raised her eyebrows, giving me a skeptical look. "No, really. You would have found it interesting as well. We had VIP passes and afterward we got to hang out with the guy who led the sessions. Really nice bloke. He's American."

"What's his name?"

"Boyd Rivers. He used to live in New York, but he operates out of Amsterdam now."

"Wow, really?"

"Yeah, he fell in love with an attorney who works there."

"Huh, an attorney and a CrossFit guru—I wonder how they met. Is she into CrossFit, too?"

"No, I think he mentioned they met through his brother, who's a musician."

"Huh. Rivers . . . it sounds familiar, but then again, it's a popular name."

"His brother is Lou Rivers, he said. Maybe you've heard of him? Boyd said he's not that famous outside the US."

"Oh, I know him! I love his music. It's a mix of folk, country, and bluegrass. He has that whole singer-songwriter thing going on. He might not be very famous, but the guy is very talented. Boyd Rivers is his brother? What are the odds!"

"It was honestly really interesting, and Mika and I learned a lot of new things. I already told Winston I can't wait to try some of these exercises in our workouts."

"Good. I'm glad you had a good weekend."

"What about you? Did you get to sleep in like you wanted?"

She scrunched up her nose and then smiled.

"No, I didn't."

"Why not?"

She hesitated for a moment and then let out a breath.

"What is it?"

"Well, it turns out I have a really hard time sleeping when I'm not curled up around my favorite human heater," she joked, but then a shy smile stretched across her face.

I didn't think—I just pulled her down to sit on top of me. I didn't care that we were in the makeup trailer with a bunch of other people. They had been busy working and minding their own business, but of course now their attention was on us. Their whistles and cheers would have embarrassed me, if I cared.

But I didn't.

"You couldn't sleep?"

"I just missed you, I suppose. I'm not used to being alone in the cottage," she replied, looking away.

I tipped her chin up and forced her to look at me. I narrowed my eyes, trying to make sure she wasn't playing.

"You missed me?" I asked her, and for some reason I couldn't stop smiling like a fool.

"Please don't make me say it again," she replied, embarrassed. "I hate when my inner Ms. Independent goes all soft. I don't mean to get mushy on you. It's good to have some time apart. Next time I will probably have no problem falling asleep."

"*Mo chridhe*, it's nothing you should be embarrassed of. It's nice to know I was missed. I missed you too."

I kissed her, slow and soft, but the whistles of the people around us reminded me once again we weren't alone. I broke the kiss unwillingly and gave her a long look, and then I turned around and gave everyone a piece of my mind.

"Shut ye geggie, ya bunch of bawbags." They all laughed at my insults, but I wasn't joking. I didn't want Nora or anyone else to hear about us making out; we had enough to deal with. "Oh, leave us alone, ya fannybaws! Don't be a wee clipe, or you'll all have to deal with me!"

Chapter 16

SAM

"You know I have a photo shoot next Friday," Hugh reminded me. We had just concluded our eighth week of shooting.

It had been a *long* day and we were finally about to head home. From time to time, we still liked to hang out in his trailer after work, because . . . I guess we were both *sentimental* about that place.

It was the same trailer he'd had the year before, after all.

Did I know he had a photo shoot? Uh, yeah.

"Oh, that's right. I had almost forgotten about that. Is it with the whole cast or just you?"

"Just me."

"Ooh la la, Mr. MacLeod. Is it going to be one of those

very fashion-forward photo shoots? Are they going to make you do crazy poses?"

He laughed, but said nothing.

"Which publication is it for? *Esquire*? *GQ*? *Entertainment Weekly*?"

He shook his head and gave me an uneasy smile. "Not really. It's a photo shoot for a clothing line."

"Which one? Any brand I know?"

"My agent told me the name, but I can't remember it right now. It's not one of the very popular ones, but it's a start, at least."

"I'm sure you'll look dashing. I can't wait to see the proofs."

"Well, actually, I was going to propose something—"

"Propose?" I deadpanned. "You've already done that."

"Har har. Different kind of proposal. Since we're off on Friday, I want you to come with me."

"Don't you think it's kind of weird that they're giving us the day off?" I said, trying to dodge his offer.

"I don't think it's weird at all. They didn't want me to miss out on this photo shoot, so they were willing to give everyone the day off."

"I'm just kind of surprised they're being so understanding about rescheduling . . . and that we are all off. Last year we still had to work even when you guys were away on the press tour."

"Well, the photo shoot is good exposure, both for me and the show. Anyway, since you don't have to work, I want you to come with me."

Act surprised.

"That's sweet, honey . . . but I'm not sure it's a good

A Scottish Wedding

idea," I said hesitantly. I really didn't want to hurt his feelings, even if it was for a greater good.

"Why not?" he asked with a tone of confusion in his voice. His eyes locked on mine. "I want you to be there for the photo shoot. You know I trust your judgment above anyone else's." His words made me smile and sent a warm rush through my body. I ran my fingers along his smooth jaw and placed a kiss on his lips.

Forget fickle Abarath—Hugh MacLeod was the dream. I hoped no one would ever discover just how dreamy he was in real life, because I wanted him all to myself. *I can't wait to marry him.* I smiled proudly, biting my bottom lip, until I remembered that I had to let him down easy.

At least momentarily.

I sighed. "That's really sweet, but they're going to have their own makeup artist."

"I don't care. I don't want you there to do my makeup, I just want *you* there."

"I would love to be there, but for one, if I do go, they'll think I'm trying to interfere with their vision—trust me, it has happened before. Photo shoots are crowded with *big egos*," I said, making a face, recalling one of Amira's first big shoots. "I went with Amira once and when I let slip I was a makeup artist, the one on the job almost threw a fit, as if I wanted to take his place. It was a miserable day for everyone. Later on, we found out there was an ongoing lovers' quarrel between the makeup artist and the photographer, so it really wasn't about me, but still, I felt horrible for my sister, because I had only gone with her to be supportive. Besides not wanting to step on anyone's toes, there's actually another reason why I can't come with you—

since we have the day off, Cecilia scheduled a spa day. I'm sorry," I told him, hoping I did sound sorry.

He frowned, disappointment clouding his eyes. "Spa day?"

"Cece claims she regrets not having a bachelorette party."

"Of course. That sounds just like something she would say," he replied.

"I know, right? She's a piece of work. She also said if we don't get pedicures we'll start looking like trolls since we are in boots twenty-four seven. I have to admit, a spa day does sound nice. I'm not totally hating the idea. I didn't think about you wanting me to tag along."

"Sam, why would I not want you around?"

"Well, I don't know. We don't have to be attached at the hip."

"It's not like we get to spend that much time together away from the set. Of course I'd want you with me, but if you're happy to go with Cecilia, it's okay with me. Unless . . . maybe you guys can reschedule for a different day?"

I looked down for a moment, unable to hold his gaze. I hated disappointing him. I hated *lying* to him—well, *half-*lying.

"I would if we could, but we're never off work during the week, you know that. We'd have to book weeks ahead to get an appointment on the weekend and there's no spa here in St. Martin. Plus, you know very well how hard it is to make Cecilia reason when she has an idea in mind. She's set on going to Edinburgh to get pampered. I'm sorry." My lies made my smile feel unnatural and I caught a worried glimpse in his eyes. I needed to do better than that. I wrapped my arms around his neck and kissed his soft lips.

"Will you be okay without me for a day?"

He nodded, but I detected a bit of reluctance in his half-smile. His eyes clouded over and he looked like he was about to say something else, but he didn't press the subject any more. I kissed him on the lips again but he barely responded, his long eyelashes concealing the skepticism in his eyes.

I decided I needed to be a little more convincing.

I leaned down and tugged the hair on the back of his neck, forcing him to look at me. I stared into his blue sapphires, meaning to say something, but I got momentarily distracted.

This season, Abarath faced several misadventures that led him to have a harsher, less manicured look than season one, meaning Hugh's hair was longer and unkempt, curls falling below his ears, and the scruff on his jaw was a bit more pronounced. Later on in the season, he'd come to sport a full beard, and I couldn't say I was too upset about it—I was actually looking forward to it. The changes suited and highlighted Hugh's features even more, particularly his high cheekbones. His eyes looked even bluer when his face was covered in "dirt," and I loved the feel of his longer, soft curls on my skin when we lay in bed together.

"I'll be back in the evening. We'll celebrate your campaign, and guess what? You'll get to enjoy the fruits of my spa day. I'm going to get a full-body exfoliation so my skin is going to be *super* soft, and you'll have me all weekend," I teased in a warm, low tone. "I'll be at your disposal—*completely*," I coaxed, arching an eyebrow. I was acting like a shameless flirt, but it was necessary.

My sexual promises broke through his icy façade and he gave me the smile I yearned for.

"Oh, you." His voice erupted from his stretched mouth with a low rumble. A shiver ran through me and soon my skin broke into goose bumps. He leaned forward to capture my mouth in a possessive hold and kissed me forcefully, as if I wasn't giving him enough of myself. The way he owned my mouth made the hair on the back of my neck stand up; my flirty words had awoken his desire. He landed his big, strong hands on my ass, forcing me to sit down on him, facing him with my legs draped on each side of his glorious body.

"This is not what I had in mind," I joked with a half-smile.

"Isn't it, now? You didn't think it through, did you? Do you think you could tease me with thoughts of your smooth, *exfoliated* body without me acting on it?" His playful tone and cocky smile were going to undermine my self-control, but I still managed to roll my eyes at him and play hard to get. Since he wasn't getting the reaction he wanted from me, the bastard started tickling me. He knew it was just a matter of seconds before I was going to beg for mercy.

And soon enough, I did. I begged him to stop as he trapped me in his arms and started covering my neck with slow-burning kisses.

"We're going to get sidetracked . . . again. By the time we get to the cottage, it's going to be late and we're not going to have any time left . . ." I mumbled in a tone that was half a plea for mercy and half encouragement for him to keep going.

"Time left for what? This?" he asked.

A Scottish Wedding

He gave my ass a squeeze with one of his hands while the other reached for one of my breasts. My body arched against his, longing, needing more of him. He ignored my words and kept exploring my skin. My body reacted like an independent being, always so ready to respond to his touch.

He ignored my plea for him to stop. Admittedly, I was not being very convincing.

"What did ye say? *All weekend long*?" The mocking, playful tone in his voice wasn't lost on me, so I kissed him again and looked straight into his eyes.

"*All* weekend. Me, you, all weekend long." That was my plan anyway.

Since we wouldn't have time to go anywhere else, a lovefest at the cottage was in order. I started trailing kisses on his neck, afraid someone would somehow come knocking on the door, even though we were done shooting for the day. I needed to get my fill of him, so I kissed him again. This time he wasn't withholding; his tongue parted my lips, wrapping around mine.

Not quite minty like he usually tasted, it was different—sweeter. He tasted like honey.

Honey.

A sudden thought crossed my mind.

"How do you say honey in Scottish?" I asked, breaking the kiss. His brows pressed together in confusion.

"Honey? Like darling? *Rùnag.*"

I smiled, thinking how much I loved the way he rolled his Rs.

"No, the honey from bees. What's it called in Scottish?"

"*Mil.*"

"*Mil*?" I repeated, and he nodded, a tight-lipped smile

on his face.

"I had some earlier. Can ye taste it?" he asked, his accent more marked on the last sentence.

"I can. You taste delicious. You always do, but this evening you're particularly sweet." I nuzzled his neck, trailing the tip of my nose on his skin, just as someone knocked on the door of the trailer.

Typical.

I let out a frustrated breath.

"I bet our driver knows we're up to no good in here," he said, but my mind was elsewhere.

"*Mil,*" I muttered under my breath and placed another kiss on his lips.

"*Mil,*" he repeated. He gave me a lingering, curious look, eyebrows drawn together. I reluctantly got up to open the door and I could feel his eyes following me across the trailer. I knew he was wondering what his brown-eyed girl could possibly have in mind.

He'll just have to wait and see.

Chapter 17

HUGH

"I just got word that the photo shoot is in Stonehaven. Are you sure you can't make it? We could try to call and make an appointment to meet the priest, see if they even have any dates available next summer. I'm sure Cecilia will have a cow, but she'll eventually understand it's important."

"Where now?" Sam asked, as if the name didn't ring a bell.

"Stonehaven, the town I told you about." Her expression was blank, her eyes drifting off as if she'd never heard the name before. She didn't remember. I couldn't believe she didn't remember. It stung. I didn't quite like the ache in my chest at the realization that she had no idea what I was talking about. I grabbed her chin and tilted it up, forcing her to look at me. Did she want to marry me or not?

I didn't want to start another argument, since every time I did bring up the wedding, she pointed out how sorely mistaken I was, how she'd been working on researching places and looking at wedding dresses, but with my schedule for next summer still up in the air, we needed to make some progress. We needed to come up with a plan.

"We don't have much time, Sam. If we don't start planning this wedding now, I don't know when we'll be able to make it happen." A long, frustrated sigh escaped my lips, and her wide brown eyes locked on mine, heavy with worry. She glanced away a couple of times, and then locked eyes with me again. Each time she seemed on the verge of saying something . . . but then she didn't.

The expression in her eyes was one I couldn't place. The only time I'd seen her this upset was when I confronted her about her past and her revenge on her ex-boyfriend, Eric. Her bottom lip trembled ever so slightly, but then she pressed her lips together and straightened herself up, as if trying to get a grip on herself. I knew I'd upset her a couple of times before with my stubbornness and jealousy, and I didn't want to do that now.

I ken I was . . . impatient, I just couldn't wait to set a date. I wanted us to have that milestone to look forward to. I didn't want other work commitments to stray us away from what we wanted, didn't want us to keep postponing it. True, we were already living together, but there was this ache in my chest, this . . . *need*. I wanted to be able to call her *my wife*. It wasn't something I could explain very well with words. It didn't make much sense to me, either—it was as if I were the victim of some kind of primordial need. It sounded positively primitive and I felt like a bawheid for just thinking about it that way. No way was I going to explain to Sam why I couldn't stop thinking about it.

My primordial, daft Neanderthal need was one reason, and work was another.

My mind went to the script in my backpack. My agent Cosima had insisted I read it, and I had. As much as I was interested in the project and wanted the role—the male lead in a thriller set in New York—I didn't want to spend the few weeks I had off from *Abarath* working on another set. The production of the movie was set to start mid-June, a timeframe we were considering for the wedding. I dismissed my thoughts about the script and the movie. I could wait to take on more roles; I couldn't wait to marry Sam.

I cradled her face in my hands and she relaxed, relishing my touch.

"Sam, look at me," I prodded. Her eyelids fluttered open and warm, brown eyes stared at me with a mix of curiosity and uncertainty. "Stonehaven is the town where they have that little church I showed you . . . the one I'd like to get married in."

Her whole face lit up, finally remembering the conversation we once had. The gorgeous smile I was familiar with stretched across her face, and I finally saw a glimpse of excitement. She wrapped her hands around my neck and my shoulders slumped, suddenly feeling more relaxed. Maybe she'd jump at the opportunity and ditch Cecilia.

Instead, her reaction and her words surprised me and confused me even more.

"Ohhhh! Right! Now I remember! You said Stonehaven and for a moment I thought the shooting was in

Stonehenge so I was confused . . . I was trying to rack my brain as to whether we had a conversation about Stonehenge."

"No, we haven't . . . as far as I can recall."

"Well, you know . . . if you wanted to get married in Stonehenge, I wouldn't be opposed to it, if you can even do such a thing. You probably can't, can you?"

"That's not even Scotland."

"Is it not?" she asked with a frown.

"No. It's England," I replied curtly.

"Ohhh! Touchy, are we? I'm sorry, all right? Forget I said anything." The pitch of her voice was higher than usual. She was nervous, and I couldn't understand why. *What is up with her today?* She seemed fidgety, so unlike herself. I kept trying to get her to look at me, but she kept looking away.

"Sam, are you okay? You're acting verra strange today."

"Y-Yes. It's just . . . I couldn't sleep last night and I overdid it with the coffee this morning. I have caffeine jitters, that's all." She shrugged and finally glanced my way for a brief moment.

"I thought you only had trouble sleeping when I was away."

"Yeah, I don't know why I couldn't sleep."

"Why didn't you wake me? I would have tried to help you go back to sleep."

"Oh, honey . . . *rùnag*," she added, smiling warmly, remembering the Scottish term of endearment. She caressed my face and brushed my hair away from my forehead. "I didn't want you to be tired today, and your photo shoot is in just a couple of days. I can afford to have bags under my eyes—you, on the other hand, cannot."

She scrunched up her nose and raised herself on her tiptoes to kiss me. There was just something about the feel of her lips under mine that always managed to ignite a chemical reaction. Each time my lips touched hers, my brain went into overdrive, telling me I needed to taste her. I had kissed her a thousand times, and each time I felt the same excitement, the same rush, the same need to taste her. Blood rushed to my head and adrenaline traveled through my veins as my tongue wrapped around hers, exploring her mouth, nipping her soft, full lips. I needed her kisses the way I needed oxygen. I craved her body the way a starving man craves food.

I wondered if this exhilarating, maddening feeling was ever going to subside. Part of me hoped it wouldn't. I wanted to love and worship her for the rest of my days.

Exhilarated and breathless from my kisses, she pulled back, sighing against my mouth.

Our foreheads touched, our noses brushing lightly.

She laughed softly.

"What's gotten into you?" she asked.

"I don't know what you're talking about."

"We're only going to be apart for twenty-four hours, MacLeod," Sam teased. "I'll be back before you know it. This might be a good chance to read the script Cosima sent you." She cocked one eyebrow, and I was suddenly taken aback.

"You knew?"

"She told me."

"She shouldn't have. Besides, it doesn't matter. I'm not doing the movie in New York."

"Like hell you aren't. You aren't going to pass this up

because of me."

"Because of . . . *us*. Besides, the role isn't even mine, and I don't intend on auditioning for it. I don't understand . . . don't you want to get married? Have you changed your mind, Sam?"

"I have not," she replied firmly. She sighed, exasperated. "Hugh, I want to marry you, and we *will* get married. We'll set a date . . . soon. As a matter of fact, let's do it as soon as I get back from my getaway. You're not passing up movie roles because we might or we might not get married around the time this movie is supposed to start shooting. I'm not letting you do this."

"But—"

"It's nonnegotiable. You'll see, everything is going to work out. Everything is going to fall into place." She placed soft, chaste kisses on my cheek.

"How do you do it?"

"Do what?"

"Butter me up like toast."

She laughed. "I swear, I'm not trying to flatter you. I just . . . *know*," she said with a coy smile. "I want to get married in Stonehaven, too. As soon as I get back, let's make a list of everything we need to do. We might have to hire a wedding planner, since we are both so busy."

"You're right. That might make things easier to handle."

"Let's start making plans . . . this weekend."

I nodded, relieved that my stupid insecurities had been washed away once more.

"So, do you know if you're going to be fully clothed for this photo shoot? Do you think there might be the chance they ask you to get naked?" She wiggled her eyebrows, and in response, I frowned.

I hadn't thought about it, at all. I had no idea what the company had in mind for the campaign, but no one had mentioned that I might have to be naked. I knew I didn't have to worry about a thing, because with the strenuous training and diet Winston had put me through, I was looking trimmer than ever. But, just like when I had to get naked on set, I couldn't help getting a little jittery.

"What's the worried look for, *mo gradh*?" Sam teased. "You'll look amazing with or without clothes on." She winked, and that made me laugh.

I was in the best shape of my life. I shouldn't have been worried. Still, even though I knew I had no reason to be nervous, I was suddenly overcome by that familiar terror of getting undressed for the camera.

SAM

I checked to make sure he was sound asleep then went downstairs to make a call.

"I almost ruined everything, Cecilia. I almost broke. I hate lying to him."

"There, there. Aren't you being a little dramatic? What brought this on?"

"He wanted me to go with him to the photo shoot, and

I . . . well, I hate disappointing him, but more than anything, I hate lying to him. You should have seen his face when I turned him down."

"You're being too hard on yourself," she said, letting out a yawn. "Go to bed, Sam."

"I can't sleep, Cece."

"Why is that?"

"I don't know." I paused. "Tell me I'm not making a colossal mistake."

"You aren't."

"That's all you've got?"

"How much more convincing do you need me to be? He's going to love it, okay? I just know it!"

"I don't trust myself."

"What do you mean?"

"I'm afraid I will let something slip. If you notice me saying something stupid tomorrow, you need to stop me and intervene. Promise me that!"

"Okay, okay, I promise." She yawned. "Now, be a good girl and go to bed. I need my beauty sleep, you know."

"Fine. Good night, Cece."

"Go to sleep, Sam."

HUGH

Sam and Cecilia left on Thursday night for their spa

A Scottish Wedding

getaway. Now it was my turn to be alone at the cottage, and I had to admit, I was feeling pretty lonely.

If I didn't have a photo shoot the next day, I would have gone into town to hang out with the guys, but I knew if I went to the pub, I'd end up getting pissed.

Makeup or not, I still had to try to look my best in the morning. I forewent the premade meals and made myself a light dinner with grilled chicken and steamed vegetables then cracked open my only indulgence of the night: a local craft beer from a brewery in Edinburgh.

Since I had some time to kill, I decided to call my brother.

"So, how you've been? How's filming going? How's Sam?" Declan asked over FaceTime.

"Good. Things on set are great, and things are good with Sam, too . . . I suppose."

"You *suppose*? Is everything okay between you two?" Declan took a swig of beer and I looked down, trying to find the right words to say.

"Yeah, things have been good, but I don't know, Declan. I know she loves me, but I keep having this ill feeling that something's wrong, that she's hiding something from me. I made an arse of myself a couple times already, and each time Sam showed me I didn't have valid reasons to be suspicious."

"I don't understand, brother. Suspicious of what?"

"I dinna ken. Sometimes I feel like maybe . . . maybe she isn't ready to get married, and I'm putting too much pressure on her."

"Well, are ye?"

I shrugged. "Sometimes, maybe. She seemed really

excited at first but lately . . . I don't know. Something is . . . off. I'd like to think by now I knew how to read her."

"Women aren't that simple, Hugh." He gave me a cocky grin, the one of someone who's been through a lot, and took another swig of his beer.

"I don't think it's a matter of *difficult* or *simple*. It's . . . something else. I think she's keeping something from me, and I can't figure out what it is."

"Have you tried talking to her without sounding like a jealous bastard? You know my marriage failed mainly because we bloody sucked at communicating what we wanted and expected from one another."

"Yeah, well . . . it's complicated, ye see. Most of the time, everything is great, but then there are some times when she tenses up . . . especially when I talk about anything wedding-related."

"So, is she scared of getting married? Is this because of her ma and da? Is it because her parents got divorced? Do you think she's getting cold feet?"

"I don't think so. She was excited, and she told me she's dress shopping and looking for suitable venues."

"It sounds to me like there's nothing you should worry about, brother. You two live *and* work together. It would be pretty hard to hide something from someone you're spending so much time with. But, if you think she doesn't want to get married any time soon, you need to ask her. Don't make the same mistake I did with my ex-wife. Talk to her."

"Ok I will, thanks. How are the kids? Are they with you? Are you even home? It doesn't look like it."

"No, I had a client and I ended up staying up here in

Edinburgh, so I'm not far from you at all. The kids are with their mum. I have them this weekend, though."

"You promised Claire you would bring them up here to visit their uncle. Don't wait too long. It won't be nearly as much fun to see the set once the temperatures go below freezing."

"You're right," my brother agreed with a grin. "I need to take them up there. I can't wait to see their faces when they see what their uncle does for a living," he teased.

"Hey!"

"All in good fun, brother. I know Claire is going to love it. Rory, on the other hand, still has a hard time understanding why there are advertisements around town with his uncle's face on it."

"Aye, I bet that's kind of weird. Sam told me that when she was little she used to think fictional characters *lived* in an alternate world, and people like her father were the ones to capture it, like a documentary of sorts."

Declan laughed, but then made a face, as if he'd suddenly thought of something.

"By the way, have you been rehearsing?" he asked.

"Yeah, well . . . I have, when she's not around. I guess it's a good thing that this year she doesn't spend that much time in my trailer. I'm always afraid she's going to catch me."

"But you have been practicing, right?" my brother asked, eyebrows raised as if he didn't believe me. "Because we don't know when it's going to be, not until you two make a decision. I would make sure you're ready."

"What are you trying to imply, brother?" I asked, feigning annoyance.

"That you should be practicing right now, since she's not around. You're not that great of a player, ye ken."

I let out a breath. It was just like an older brother to tell you what to do at any given time, or tell you flat-out how shit you were at something.

"Fine," I replied. "I'll get the guitar out."

"That's a good lad. I'll go get mine and we can practice together."

I was grumpy when I woke up in the morning.

Declan and I practiced for a couple of hours and I ended up having two more beers.

As soon as I opened my eyes, I brought a hand down to my stomach. I hoped I wasn't going to feel bloated today; I had to look my best. I stretched out my hand to Sam's side, and only then remembered she was gone.

I sighed.

Not only did I miss my brown-haired siren, I was starting to feel a bit resentful.

I hadn't heard from her at all, and even though I knew she and Cecilia had all kinds of pampering lined up, I thought I'd get a few messages or a FaceTime call from her.

Even so, I knew nothing good came from being jealous and clingy, knew I had to give her space, so I took a shower in the hope of washing away my sour mood.

I started feeling a bit better when I got in the car and drove toward Stonehaven.

A Scottish Wedding

I had visited this town many times as a kid, and I loved the little church by the cliff. I made a mental note to go by there, since we were supposed to shoot not far from there.

Maybe next time Sam and I would be able to visit together and start planning our wedding. I didn't want to rush her, but I couldn't wait to see her in a billowy white dress, walking down the aisle to the sound of "Wedding March."

I kept fantasizing about us, together, on our wedding night.

When I got to town, I realized just how close to the church the location of the photo shoot was.

I took a quick picture and sent it to Sam.

A few seconds later, she replied with a message.

Oh, my goodness. It's just as beautiful as you said.

It's pretty, isn't it?

That's a killer panorama. Fine, you convinced me. I'm sold. We either marry at this place or nowhere else!

Well, don't be so dramatic now. If this place is not available any time soon, we'll find something else, maybe something even better.

Whatever you say, love. I miss you. Sorry I didn't call you last night. I was pretty much babysitting Cecilia as she worshipped the ceramic

God.

You're kidding.

No, unfortunately. But I have a massage in five, so my day is fixing to get a lot better. How's the photo shoot going?

We haven't started yet. They are getting me ready. Also, you'll love this: the shoot is for a company specialized in Scottish formalwear.

Sounds like they got the best testimonial they could ask for. I need to go now! Don't forget to turn that smolder on for the camera! Love you!

I shot her a quick reply and then relaxed in the makeup chair, even though it felt weird and different not having her around. She'd said she was sorry she couldn't call; my brother was right—Sam wasn't hiding anything from me.

I was just overreacting and being a stubborn arse.

Chapter 18

HUGH

Over the next two hours, I changed outfits four times. They took pictures of me in the courtyard by the church in different combinations of formal attire, the kind a groom would wear during his wedding. The photographer also decided to take some pictures by the ruins of the old church, and the view from that angle was simply stunning.

I wore different combinations of jackets and tartans, and for my fourth outfit, they dressed me in familiar colors. I was wearing the MacLeod tartan.

It had to be a coincidence.

This suit had a more modern twist compared to the one I wore for Declan's wedding. It was more like what I had seen my peers wear—the tartan paired with a dark shirt—instead of the more classic black jacket and white button-down.

When I saw myself in the mirror, I took a deep breath, admiring the craftsmanship and how well it fit me. I wished Sam could see me. *Oh well.* She would see it soon enough when they sent the proofs over, and then it hopefully wouldn't be too long before she saw me in an outfit like this one in person.

I walked with the photographer, Arnauld, and his assistants back to the front of the church.

"Let's take some pictures inside the church now," the photographer suggested.

I frowned. "Is that even allowed?" I asked.

"Oh, *oui, mon ami*. We asked permission ahead of time," he said with his French accent. "But I need to take a little break, and I also need to change cameras. Go ahead and wait for me inside. Sandra will escort you," he said, pointing at one of his assistants. They were all young women in their twenties, petite, dressed in black, and each wearing a headset. Sandra was speaking into the microphone of her headset and clutching a plain black clipboard to her chest when her boss called her over.

"Sandra, *ma chere*! Accompany Hugh into the church, s'il vous plaît?"

I nodded, still a bit perplexed.

"Mr. MacLeod, please follow me."

"You can call me Hugh," I said with a perplexed frown.

"Is everything okay, Hugh?" Sandra asked.

"Yeah. It's just . . ." I let out a small laugh. "I just don't understand what the point of having three assistants around is if Arnauld is going to do everything on his own—changing cameras and things like that, I mean."

A Scottish Wedding

"Oh, well, you see, Arnauld is very controlling, especially when it comes to his equipment. Those are his toys. He calls the cameras *mon petit chou*," she said, snickering. "Get it? He calls the cameras *darlings*. He won't let any of us touch them. Oh, this church is so pretty!" Sandra exclaimed as she opened the side door of the church and let me in.

I looked toward the altar and crossed myself as I had been taught when I was a wee lad. I lifted my eyes after bowing in the direction of the altar and took a look around. Sandra was right; the church was pretty. It was small, but cozy. It was as beautiful as I remembered, although now that I was a grown man, I realized I remembered it bigger than it actually was. Even so, I knew that wouldn't be an issue, because Sam and I both wanted a small wedding.

The church was simple with bare stone walls and small glass windows depicting the life of Jesus Christ. It wasn't overly ornate, but it had character.

I knew this had to be the place.

I noticed that because of the narrow, gothic style windows, there wasn't much light. "It's so dark. How are we going to take pictures in here?" I asked her.

"Yeah, I know," she agreed. "We're going to need some light in here. I'm going to grab some equipment outside. Wait here, okay?"

I nodded and started walking around, admiring the space.

There was something rather solemn about walking around in an empty church, as if you were on the verge of having a private audience with God himself.

I started noticing small details here and there. There

were white flowers on the altar, and similar bouquets with green and blue ribbons decorated the edges of the wooden benches along the nave.

Maybe they just had a wedding . . . but we had been there for hours and I hadn't seen anyone come or go. *Maybe they had one yesterday.* I took a closer look at one of the bouquets: it had small white roses mixed with baby's breath, lily of the valley, white freesia flowers, and something else I couldn't recognize.

Then my eyes fell on the freesia flower again, because it reminded me of Sam. It was one of her favorite flowers.

I walked back to the altar again, still alone in the church, my stomach in knots for some reason I couldn't articulate. I wondered if I was going to feel more nervous than I did right then on my wedding day.

Maybe it was just that being here, in a place I loved, dressed in formal wear, only heightened my desire and eagerness to get married.

I looked up at the altar, and I stared at the effigy of Christ sitting over the tabernacle. I closed my eyes for a few seconds.

Everything was so eerily quiet. You could have heard a pin drop.

Suddenly, I was startled by some noises coming from outside, and I turned around as the doors of the church opened with a loud thud.

SAM

Call me an international woman of mystery. For the

A Scottish Wedding

last two months, I had been planning a wedding under the nose of my unsuspecting fiancé.

Sure, there were a few close calls—his suspicions and jealousy about Fern, for starters. I couldn't believe how worked up he got about that.

Totally unnecessary.

Or the subtle grief he gave me for wanting to go to a spa with Cecilia instead of coming to his "photo shoot."

Again, completely uncalled for.

"Oh, Sam! You look beautiful! Hugh's jaw is going to drop. Fern said they're almost ready for us. You need to sit tight for a few more minutes," Amira told me, opening the door of the car.

Hugh had absolutely no need to get upset about Fern . . . my handsome and charming *wedding planner*. I hoped the "fake photo shoot" crew was filming every moment of this, because I hated to miss out on Hugh's reaction as the church filled with our closest friends and family members.

It hadn't been easy, but with the help of my allies, I had been able to pull this off.

In just a few minutes, I'd be walking down the aisle. My dad was going to put my hand in Hugh's, and in about an hour, we'd be husband and wife. The priest, Father Adams, had warned me that the Catholic wedding rite was *long* and didn't happen as fast as it did in those American movies—his words.

Obviously, I didn't have enough time to convert to Catholicism. Father Adams made it clear when I met with him that he would have preferred it, especially since I hadn't been raised in any particular religion, but I'd explained to him that we wanted to get married sooner rather than later.

The Scottish priest was not enthusiastic about my plan. It had taken a few calls and a few words from Hugh's parents during the last few weeks to convince him to officiate a surprise wedding. Apparently, in Scotland, it was actually against the law to have one.

In the end, Father Adams reluctantly agreed to my request, though not before telling me he would require the groom's approval to proceed before officiating the ceremony.

He was as curious as he was baffled by my plans.

Admittedly, it was unusual, but to be honest, I had been wanting to surprise Hugh ever since he left me speechless with his swoon-worthy proposal. I had known almost immediately that somewhere down the road, I had to reciprocate with a gesture just as grand as his.

When we started filming, it became evident that he was never going to have time to plan the wedding with me. We could have set the date for the next summer, but I knew he was going to be gone a lot promoting the show, and I didn't want him to miss out on possible side projects. The more I thought about a wedding the next summer, the more it sounded unlikely. With the show's filming schedule lasting anywhere from six to eight months, his free time was limited.

I loved him, and I wanted him to be able to make his dreams come true.

That included our nuptials, as well as his career.

He had been waiting to get more opportunities for over a decade, so I didn't want him to miss out on the good ones now that they had started to arrive. Unlike him, I had been working steadily since I'd gotten out of school. I never really knew struggle when it came to my profession, and now I had the job of a lifetime. I didn't see being supportive as a duty; I saw it as a natural trait of a healthy relationship. I knew he would do the same for me.

"Are you doing okay, honey?" my dad asked, squeezing my hand, interrupting my daydream.

"I think so. So far, at least." I smiled, but as the words left my lips, I felt my stomach fill with butterflies. An uneasy feeling crept up all the way to my chest, clutching my heart.

Suddenly, I felt a knot in my throat.

Am I doing the right thing? Is he going to react the way I hope?

I turned around to ask my dad, but he let himself out of the car at just that moment.

Get your shit together, Samhain. Too late to go back now.

Amira reappeared and opened the door of the black Mercedes.

I took a deep breath and extended my hand out to her.

"Wait!" she whispered. "Oh, my gosh! Where's your something blue? You have something new," she said, pointing at my dress.

I let out a laugh. She was going to like this.

"Mira . . ." I pursed my lips in a smile.

"Your engagement ring is your something old, my necklace is your something borrowed . . . but what about your something blue?"

"Mira!" I said again, trying to get her attention, but she wouldn't stop rambling.

"How could we forget this? I'm the worst maid of honor ever!"

"Mira, would you listen to me? We're fine." She had left the spa before I was ready in order to go over the last few things with Fern and Declan, another one of my accomplices, so she hadn't seen me with my dress on . . . or my shoes.

I pulled up a bit of my dress, turned in my seat, and stretched my legs out of the car, showing her my feet, clad in blue leather flats.

"Here's my something blue."

"You're wearing flats on your wedding day?"

"Why not? I'd rather dance all night than not enjoy my wedding because my feet are killing me."

"What's the holdup?" Cecilia asked as she walked toward us. She'd been waiting by the entrance of the church and out of the corner of my eye, I saw her growing more impatient by the second.

"Nothing. Mira wanted to make sure I had everything I needed. I do." I glanced at the two of them, clad in similar hunter green, floor-length chiffon dresses. They were holding small bouquets with heather, lily of the valley, and baby's breath, tied together with ribbons the colors of the MacLeod tartan.

"You both look beautiful."

Amira smiled while Cecilia said, "Of course we do! Do you think I could look less than *simply stunning*, especially next to Ms. Hollywood right here?" she said, pointing at my sister.

"Ah, stop it!" Amira said with a wave of her hand. "You look gorgeous, Cece."

"Thank you, ma'am. Now, are we bloody done? Your groom must be wondering what the hell is going on."

I smiled, somewhat nervous but mostly ready to cross the threshold of the church and see my man at the altar.

"Jolly good! If that isn't the smile of a radiant bride, I don't know what it is. Hugh's jaw is going to drop. You look so beautiful!"

I mumbled, "Thank you," and squeezed her hand.

"Come on, you three," our father admonished us. "It's time to go. Your groom is waiting." He tilted his head toward the church and gave me a reassuring smile then stretched his hand out to help me out of the car. Amira grabbed my bouquet and Cecilia helped me with the veil as I came out of the sleek car.

All around us, the invitees were lining up to take their seats in the church and give my groom one hell of a surprise. I caught a few glimpses of some of our family members and coworkers.

Amira and Cecilia fixed my dress and waited for people to make their way in before they lined up behind Rory and Claire.

"Ready to go?" My father smiled at me and patted my hand where it rested in the crook of his elbow.

I nodded, smiling nervously. This was happening. I couldn't wait to see Hugh's face.

HUGH

Everything had been so quiet in the church, and then all of a sudden, it wasn't.

The doors opened, and a commotion broke the austere silence.

Half of the nave of the church was flooded in light, and I squinted, my eyes trying to adjust. People started making their way through the doors. Still blinded by the light, I couldn't make out their faces, could only see their silhouettes.

Are we interrupting a wedding? The church's staff would have told us if we were . . . wouldn't they?

In the distance, outside in the courtyard, I could barely make out the silhouette of a woman in white holding the arm of a man dressed in black.

My eyes were glued to the woman, because from a distance, she looked eerily familiar. *But it can't be, can it? It isn't possible. It can't be Sam.* She'd told me she had plans for the day.

Unless . . .

I scanned for the crew from the photo shoot, but I couldn't see them anywhere. I looked toward the exit where the woman had stood just a moment before, but I lost sight of her as more attendees made their way into the church. As people came forward and took their seats, I recognized some familiar faces—people from the crew, supporting actors . . . my Uncle Finley and my Aunt Flora.

I waved at them, dumbfounded.

Wait a minute . . .

A voice inside me told me to keep calm, but I couldn't. I needed to know. Was this it? Was this *my* wedding? How could this be true? I was frozen on the spot for a few more seconds before I decided to make my way through the family members who waved at me as they entered through the narrow doors of the church.

I wasn't sure how I was going to navigate through the

incoming crowd, but I had to try. I started marching toward the exit until I felt someone pulling my arm.

"That's not how it's supposed to work, ya ken. You need to wait for her to come to ye," my brother Declan said with a smug grin.

I smiled, surprised to see him, and then frowned, still confused. My brother turned me around and pulled me into a hug. I hardly reciprocated it, stunned by the fact that he was in front of me—it meant this was probably *my* wedding.

"Declan, what the bloody hell is going on?" I asked, still sort of confused about the whole thing. I had left my house that morning thinking I was headed for a photo shoot, but now I was about to get married?

How? How had she orchestrated all of this? How had she had the time to organize a wedding in . . . what, two months?

"What do ye think is going on, brother? It's your wedding day. Smile." He grinned, patting my cheek with a heavy hand.

I let out a deep breath and smiled, but it felt forced. I was still deeply confused about how I'd found myself at the center of a surprise wedding.

A surprise wedding *my fiancée* organized.

That vixen.

"Come," my brother said, motioning for me to join him by the altar where our younger brothers were waiting for us, all dressed in attire identical to mine. As I scanned my brother's figure, I reckoned it wasn't the same jacket and kilt he'd worn at his own wedding years ago. This one was a dark blue with a modern, fitted cut, and it covered the hips. The shirt was a dark blue like the one I was wearing. Even the tie matched the blue of the jacket and the shirt, and it had a little tie clip with our clan's colors. The tartan's colors were undoubtedly those of the MacLeod clan, but the style of the kilt seemed slightly different from the one I'd worn at Declan's wedding.

As I walked back to the altar, I noticed my relatives sitting down on one side of the church as my parents approached, as well as Sam's mother and brother.

"Mum! Dad!" I said with a nervous wave before my mother wrapped me in a tight hug.

"You look very handsome!" my mum said as she kissed my cheek. I nodded, but couldn't come up with anything to say. It was obvious they were all part of the surprise. My father patted me on the back.

"Hey, Dad." My voice came out in a whisper as we hugged. They told me not to be nervous and took their seats.

Sam's mother hugged me next.

"You had no idea, did you?" she asked. Kathleen seemed a bit stunned herself. The amused look in her eyes told me she also couldn't believe her daughter had kept all this under wraps, right under my nose. I let out a breath and shook my head no, still having trouble formulating complete sentences.

"Well, I couldn't be happier to gain such a handsome and devoted son-in-law. I couldn't imagine a better man for my little girl." She caressed my cheek, and then it was Rob's turn to say hello.

Rob looked like a taller version of Sam's father—I had seen pictures of the man when he was younger—but unlike his dad, he had a cooler, more distant demeanor. Rob was an app developer, and as the brainiac of the family, he was the observant, contemplative one. We'd had very little chance to hang out, even when I was in the States with Sam, so I felt I didn't know him that well yet. Sam, Amira, and I worked in the same industry, while Rob's social circle was in Silicon Valley. We fist bumped and hugged the way American blokes did with their friends. He took a seat with my future mother-in-law and I turned around to say hi to a few friends and colleagues.

Everyone was all smiles while I probably looked like a frazzled mess of a man.

Declan tugged on my sleeve to pull me where I was supposed to stand near the altar and my brothers took turns giving me hugs. Seeing them all there with me made me feel grounded, although my head was still spinning. *How did she pull this off?*

"Stop acting all out of sorts, Hugh. Now's the time to put those acting skills to good use, brother."

"You're right," I replied with a nod, taking a deep breath.

"You're marrying a bonnie lass who's mad for you."

I nodded again, still lost in my thoughts. My heart was beating a million beats per minute, and although it wasn't particularly warm inside the church, I felt sweat trickle down the back of my neck. I brushed a strand of hair to the side and ran my hand down my face, telling myself to stop being such a flap.

As the last few guests took their seats, a string quartet started playing in a corner by the altar. I was momentarily distracted by it, until I saw Claire and Rory at the entrance of the church.

Rory came down the aisle first, carrying the rings on a

wee pillow. He stopped midway and looked back to his sister, the uncertain look in his eyes betraying his confusion. When bossy little Claire mouthed not so quietly to, "*Keep going*," the whole congregation erupted in laughter. When Rory neared the altar, my mum took his hand and guided him to sit with her. Claire came down the nave of the church next, throwing white rose petals with a confidence I'd never seen in a child her age.

After Claire, it was Cecilia and Amira's turn. They both walked slowly, and as they made their way toward the altar, I tried to get a better look at my bride.

I nodded hello to Cecilia first and then to Amira.

Finally, the woman I love made her way down the aisle, accompanied by her father.

SAM

I had been so sure of everything. I hadn't had a doubt about it.

Not once.

Until now.

I didn't know why I had started feeling insecure about it for the first time ever as I stepped out of the car, but the ache clutching my heart had only intensified since then.

My arm was wrapped around my father's as we waited for our turn to cross the threshold of the church.

I had been so impatient about it all.

I couldn't wait to see his face, his reaction.

But now, the certainty I'd had about it had vanished, replaced by a million insecurities.

A Scottish Wedding

What if he hated this? What if he thought this was nothing but a crass manipulation at his expense? What if he felt betrayed because of what I'd kept from him?

What if he hated my idea? Would he end up hating me?

What if he walked out on me?

This was stupid. I shouldn't have gotten so carried away—and why did everyone else get on board with this insane plan? I was losing it, and I was all too aware that it was too late to go back.

What the fuck have I done?

"Fuck," I muttered under my breath, and my father heard me.

He cocked one eyebrow at me, giving me one of those looks he reserved for when I really misbehaved.

"Sam, language. We're about to enter a church after all, and you're about to get married—in front of God, in his house. Have some respect."

"Yes, Dad," I said, pursing my lips.

Cecilia had just walked down the aisle, and Amira had just started walking toward the altar. I couldn't see very well from where we were standing.

I swallowed past the knot in my throat and let out a deep breath, trying to calm my nerves. My father noticed and patted the hand that was wrapped around his arm.

"It's only normal to feel nervous, my dear."

"It's not just that, Dad. Are you sure I didn't make a colossal mistake?"

He eyed me suspiciously and gave me a bitter look.

"It's a bit too late to get cold feet, Sam."

"I don't have cold feet. I still want *this* very much, but what if he doesn't? What if he hates all of it?"

My dad laughed softly, his eyes crinkling at the corners, and shook his head.

"No, he won't. He's not going to hate it, not if he loves you as much as I think he does. Besides, most grooms would be perfectly happy to have no part in wedding planning. Most grooms would be happy with just being asked to show up."

I smiled at his words, but I wasn't completely convinced. Hugh was not "most grooms." He'd always given me the impression he wanted to be part of the process.

And I had taken that away from him.

"Sam, just stop second-guessing yourself," my father said. "Everything will be okay, I promise you."

I gave him a tight-lipped smile and took another deep breath.

I tried to focus, but my stupid thoughts wouldn't leave me alone.

"Come on, we're up next," my father said.

I swallowed again and let my father lead me, stepping on the first step of the church. It would have been easier if I could have seen his face then.

If I could have seen his eyes, could have seen his smile, or simply studied his reaction, I would have been okay.

But I couldn't really see him from where I was standing.

The church, built in the late 1800s, had a vaguely gothic style, that austere look many churches around Scotland and England have. I wasn't an expert, but like I said, I'd done a bit of research. The church was all high arches and bare walls, made of simple stone, with small, pointy windows along the sides. There were more windows behind the altar, but it still didn't provide enough light for me to be able to look in from where I was.

Also, I could barely see because of another reason—it was a bright and sunny day.

Scotland weather always knew how to surprise me.

It had to be sunny today of all days, when I had kind of been wishing for some rain, just for good luck.

Oh well.

"It's showtime, Samhain," my father said as the song I had chosen to walk down the aisle to started. It was my cue to get to the entrance of the church as my bridesmaids took their place by the altar.

I was uncertain as I took my first step—despite the flats—and I gripped my father's arm tighter. As we crossed the entrance of the church, everyone stood up, and the drumming of my heart became so loud, I could feel it all the way in my ears.

In that moment, I could only focus on my breath, and on the fact that the man I love was only a few steps away.

I looked ahead of me and spotted his silhouette by the altar.

I still couldn't see his face, but one thing gave me certainty: I couldn't wait to see his smile again. It was the only thing that might be able to ground me.

HUGH

My eyes hadn't left her since she'd appeared with her father at the entrance of the church. The nervousness I had initially felt was trading places with a different feeling.

It was astonishment mixed with sheer happiness.

I still couldn't believe we were here and this was happening.

I couldn't believe she had made all this happen.

She took a few more steps, and as she got closer, our eyes locked.

I smiled at her as tears started pricking my eyes. I blinked them away, hoping I'd be able to keep my emotions under wrap. Good God, she looked beautiful. She was always beautiful in my eyes, but there was just something about seeing her all dressed in white.

She looked ethereal, entirely too beautiful and perfect for this earth.

As she got closer, she returned my smile, erasing any feeling of uneasiness.

I suddenly remembered why we were here. There was absolutely no need to be nervous. We were here because she was my happiness.

She was my present, my future, my entire world. I'd wanted to marry her long before the day I proposed to her, and even though she had given me quite the shock with this surprise wedding, I couldn't wait for the priest to pronounce us husband and wife.

As she got closer, I got to appreciate how stunning she looked. She was wearing a long veil that covered her face, but I could still see her beaming smile through it. Her dress was a soft shade of white, with off-the-shoulder long sleeves and a slight V-neck in the middle. The skirt of the dress was wide, but the top of it hugged her curves in all the right places and made her look like a goddess.

My goddess.

A Scottish Wedding

My Samhain.

I swallowed, taking her beauty in as my heart started thundering inside my chest once again. I couldn't remember my heart beating so fast and so hard ever before. It was as if I could feel it in every inch, every single cell of my body.

I wanted to remember this moment for the rest of my life.

The string quartet played a song that sounded eerily familiar, but I couldn't place it right on the spot. Then, I noticed my fiancée mouthing the words of the song.

I remembered it then.

It was a song that talked about promises and spending the rest of our lives together.

SAM

Strangely enough, I couldn't find someone who could sing the more classic "Ave Maria" at the wedding—organizing a wedding on a whim had taught me I had to be *very* flexible. In the end, I hired a string quartet to perform a few songs. I debated going for a more classic, religious piece, but ultimately, I choose otherwise. When I made the list of the songs I wanted the band to play, I came across U2's "All I Want Is You."

It seemed such a perfect choice. The original arrangement relied heavily on strings and I just knew it would sound beautiful played by a string quartet, especially with the nice acoustics the church provided.

Step after step, I knew I had to focus on one thing and one thing only.

Him.

The thought of him was the only thing that would make me not lose my grip.

I mouthed the lyrics, eyes fixed on Hugh. I was trying to focus on the music, because as I entered the church, I was overcome once again by the enormity of this.

Did I go about this all wrong? I must have lost my mind to think he'd be okay with this. Why did no one try to stop me from making such a terrible mess of things?

I had been so sure of everything, but as I walked toward him, I was riddled with self-doubt—not about the wedding, but about the way I'd handled things.

Hugh looked so tall and handsome in his Scottish wedding outfit, and it took my breath away. The expression on his face was serious and solemn. I exhaled, trying to steady myself, bracing for the worst.

He hates my surprise.

But just then, his serious gaze gave way to a face-splitting grin that illuminated his whole countenance. If he had looked handsome before with his stoic demeanor, it was nothing compared to how he looked when he was smiling at me. His eyes were brilliant sapphires, sparkling with joy.

He was breathtaking. Simply breathtaking.

If I had been on the verge of tears before because of my nerves, it was nothing compared to how I felt now that I'd gotten the reaction I was hoping for.

I smiled back, lips trembling as the knot in my throat threatened to open the waterworks. It was all too much—the music, the place, the smell of the flowers, the expression in his eyes. My mouth went dry, and my heart went into overdrive.

A Scottish Wedding

Oh, the way his eyes regarded me. The look on his face was one I didn't remember ever having seen before. A mixture of love and pride, and a slight nervousness that made him look vulnerable and possibly even more handsome. The corners of his mouth curled up in the most delicious half-smile and my heart nestled in my throat, thumping merrily as I began feeling swept away by a cyclone of emotions.

I knew I was getting carried away, and we hadn't even begun yet.

I was determined to make it tear-free until the end of the ceremony.

I had to keep my head level—I didn't want to be one of those weepy brides that can't make it through their vows without sobbing.

I had to be *strong*.

Yes, you can relish this moment, but don't get carried away.

Besides, I had to be the steady one. I had thrown my groom such a curveball with this surprise wedding, it wouldn't be fair if I turned out to be the emotional one.

I had known this was coming.

He, on the other hand, didn't have a clue.

By some kind of miracle, I was able to stop the internal madness right before I reached the point of no return.

I noticed Hugh's fists clench and tighten as if he were as impatient as I was to reach the altar and take my place next to him.

My love stood tall next to his four handsome brothers, his kilt bearing the colors of his clan, the dark blue jacket highlighting his wide shoulders and impressive physique.

Hugh's hair was slightly messy and unruly, just how I liked it. I was happy the styling team hadn't messed with it during the *fake* photo shoot.

As I took a few more steps, his lips parted, eyes beaming with wonder. I watched him watch me as I approached the altar and stole a quick glance when my father lifted the veil. My dad kissed me on the cheek and when he pulled back, my self-control wavered at the sight of his eyes brimming with tears.

"I love you, Daddy." My voice was low and raspy, heavy with emotion.

"I love you too, sweetheart." He squeezed the hand that had been holding his arm, and after exchanging a quick hug with my groom, my father placed the same hand in the clasp of my soon-to-be-husband. I looked up at my groom just as a small smile stretched on his beautiful face, his bright blue eyes betraying emotions similar to my own.

"How is this for soon?" I managed to ask as he leaned in to kiss the hand he was holding.

Chapter 19

SAM

"Sam." His voice was low and gravelly, his eyes as bright as burning stars. His lips touched my skin, and a shiver ran down my arm. He locked his gaze with mine, and the way he regarded me made me . . . *thirsty*.

"Sam, it's . . . perfect. You look *stunning*. You'll have to forgive me, but I am momentarily dazed."

I let out a laugh, surprised by his formal tone, and that helped ease the tension in my stomach.

"You look very handsome yourself."

"Thank you," he replied with a slight nod of his head. He held my hand in his, standing next to me, his eyes taking in every detail of my appearance as we waited for the string quartet to finish playing. The priest, Father Adams, was right behind the altar with a solemn, unreadable expression on his face. Hugh glanced at my veil, looked at my face, and scanned down to the deep V of my dress. He met my eyes again and winked.

"You didn't just do that, did you?" I teased, leaning toward him.

"Samhain, I'm having a very hard time not having impure thoughts right now, and you're not helping."

I scoffed in disbelief.

"Why don't you tell me how ye could pull this off, instead?" His eyes narrowed on me, eyebrows pulled together, just as the priest asked everyone to take a seat as we were about to start. I pursed my lips together, trying to contain my excitement, and I gave him a nonchalant shrug.

"You're not the only one capable of grand gestures, Hugh MacLeod."

The smile that stretched across his face made my breath hitch, and the look he gave me was one I wanted to see for the rest of my life. He was beaming with happiness and pride, and I couldn't wait to make him as happy as he made me. I couldn't wait to make him happy for the rest of my days, till death do us part.

"Samhain," he whispered, looking into my eyes, his mouth less than an inch from my face, "I can't wait for the priest to declare us husband and wife."

I smiled playfully, blood rising to my cheeks, unable to resist his relentless flirting. Just then Father Adams cleared his throat, and when we looked his way, he raised his eyebrows at us, silently asking us to behave with that certain look ordained ministers seem to master so well.

"Since this is a rather unusual wedding, I want to make sure both parties are willing to enter into the covenant of

A Scottish Wedding

Holy Matrimony. I especially want to make sure the groom is in agreement, since this wedding ceremony was a surprise sprung on him by his bride-to-be." Father Adams smiled, making his words a tad bit sweeter.

Everyone laughed, including Hugh.

"Hugh, are you here to take this woman in Holy Matrimony?"

"I am," my groom replied with a dashing smile, and butterflies swarmed around in my stomach. He smiled sweetly, lifting my hand so he could kiss it again. Warmth rushed through my chest, all the way up to my cheeks.

I, the blushing bride, couldn't stop smiling.

Ever since that day in Edinburgh when we couldn't get our marriage license, I had been waiting for a way to surprise the man I loved. I wanted to show him just how much his dreams mirrored mine.

"Let's get started," Father Adams said, bringing me out of my daydream. "I know not everyone here today is familiar with the Catholic rite of marriage, so I will try to keep it as simple as possible." He then started the ceremony with a prayer.

Next Hugh's Aunt Flora read the first reading, his brother Ewan read the Psalm, and his mother Fiona read the second reading. She cast a loving look upon the two of us before taking her place at the small pulpit of the church. Hugh and I joined hands, and I heard his sharp intake of breath as his mother took the podium. For someone like me, everything about this was foreign, and there was something mystical and fascinating in all the little details of the ceremony.

As she read from a letter of Saint Paul to the Romans,

she often looked toward us. "Welcome one another as Christ welcomed you,' she recited.

Hugh started fidgeting with my hand, which I found adorable.

Emotions were flying high all around us.

Fiona's voice was tense and full of emotion as she read the passage, but she tried to slow herself to keep her voice steady. She managed well, only wavering toward the end, drying the corners of her eyes when she was done.

She and her son exchanged a smile, and then her eyes were on me, nodding in approval. Fiona had been such a great help planning this wedding; I couldn't have done it without her.

After the second reading, we had the gospel, and then Father Adam's homily, which focused on the importance and the sacredness of marriage, on how no one should enter this sacrament without being completely sure of their commitment.

Father Adams looked at Hugh again, as if wanting to give him another way out, which made me want to roll my eyes. As much as I appreciated the priest's cooperation, his diffidence was rather upsetting. I wasn't trying to nail the man to a cross, after all. I simply wanted to start our life as a married couple sooner rather than later.

Then, it was finally time to exchange vows.

As much as I'd tried to tell myself to stay calm, my heart had been hammering incessantly in my chest, the sound of it so powerful, it nearly overpowered the priest's voice. My right hand was still connected to Hugh's left—he hadn't let go of it since the ceremony had started. He looked so handsome in his attire, and every time he looked at me

A Scottish Wedding

and smiled, his eyes crinkled at the corners in that way that was so familiar. The corners of his lips curled up and my stomach did a little somersault.

I couldn't wait to be able to kiss him properly without causing a scandal.

By the time Father Adams started with the vows, my brain could only perceive bits and pieces. I had remained steady for as long as I could, but now I could feel myself crumbling.

"Since it is your intention to enter into the covenant of Holy Matrimony, join your right hands and declare your consent before God and his Church," Father Adams said.

He paused, and then he looked to my groom. "Hugh, repeat after me."

Hugh nodded, and then the priest started reciting the vows.

"I, Hugh MacLeod, take you, Samhain Farouk, to be my wife. I promise to be true to you in good times and in bad, in sickness and in health. I will love and honor you for all the days of my life."

I held my breath as he said the words. There was a severity in his expression, and the tone of his voice was as stoic as I'd often heard it on set. His eyes burned with the same fire I had seen many times before. There was also a certain sweetness in them as he promised to love me and honor me for the rest of his life.

The way he looked at me, the way he sounded as he recited the vows made me waver. I felt tears pool in the corners of my eyes just as Father Adams was calling my name.

I swallowed past the knot in my throat, took a deep

breath, and smiled. I tried to make it through my vows slowly, without rushing the words, hoping I could make them sound as beautiful and solemn as he had.

"I, Samhain Farouk, take you, Hugh MacLeod, to be my husband. I promise to be faithful to you in good times and in bad, in sickness and in health. I will love and honor you for all the days of my life."

"May I have the rings, please?"

Rory, guided by Declan, came forth. He handed Father Adams the pillow with the rings, and the priest blessed them with holy water. Father Adams instructed Hugh as to what to say, and he repeated the words right after.

"Sam, take this ring as a sign of my love and fidelity, in the name of the Father, of the Son, and of the Holy Spirit." His voice wavered, and when I looked into his eyes, I noticed he was trying to rein in his emotions just as I had moments before. He gave me a half-smile, and I responded with the same mix of excitement and nervousness.

He slipped the simple gold band on my finger, and then it was my turn to say the words.

"Hugh, take this ring as a sign of my love and fidelity, in the name of the Father, of the Son, and of the Holy Spirit."

"Lord, bless and consecrate this groom and bride in their love for each other. May these rings be a symbol of their true faith in each other, and always remind them of their love through Christ our Lord. By the powers vested in me by God, I now pronounce you husband and wife."

Father Adams hadn't even finished declaring us Mr. and Mrs. before Hugh's lips were on mine, taking me a little by surprise. In the midst of everyone cheering and clapping, his hands wrapped around my waist, bringing me closer to

A Scottish Wedding

him. My hands cradled his face as his kiss transformed into something deeper, more suited for a movie set than a church ceremony. Father Adams cleared his throat and tapped him on the shoulder when Hugh didn't budge.

"Aye, son. That's enough. Remember you're in the house of Jesus Christ."

Hugh pulled back, giving the priest a quick nod.

"Sorry, Father," he said in a raspy tone.

He straightened himself up and rewarded me with a wicked gleam and that impenitent grin I loved so much.

It was my turn to hold back.

I very much wanted to kiss him again, but the ceremony was far from over.

There was the communion consecration, the prayer, the communion itself, and the post-communion hymn and prayer.

All that meant that besides holding hands and staring at each other impatiently, there was not much else we could do. For the rest of the ceremony, Hugh tried his best to conceal his restlessness, but I knew him well enough to understand that he was having a hard time containing himself, just as I was. He suddenly had restless leg syndrome and kept fidgeting in his seat.

Toward the end of the ceremony, after the communion rite was over, he leaned toward me.

"Samhain, did I tell you how beautiful you look?"

I nodded, trying to contain a laugh.

"You did."

"I'm having the hardest time rejecting impure thoughts right now, ye ken."

"Shhh, I don't want Father Adams to reprimand us

again."

My eyes scanned his handsome face, his tartan-clad figure, and then fell to his bare knees. He cleared his throat, urging me to bring my eyes back to his. He gave me a long look, eyebrows raised, as if he were trying to communicate something without words. He gave me another panty-melting grin and I blushed, wondering if this time he was being *traditional* about the kilt.

He nodded, as if he knew exactly what I was thinking.

I felt my cheeks heat up even more. Yes, I did feel bad having such thoughts in a place of worship, but I couldn't help it.

"Ye see, the stylist didn't give me anything to wear . . . *under*. It's a wee . . . *cold*, I must admit." The corner of his lips tilted up, and the spark in his eyes made my heart throttle in my chest.

"Oh my gosh, stop it. You are so bad!" I said, pursing my lips to hold back a laugh. He reached for my hand and I swatted it away playfully.

"I thought you might want to know," he teased, completely shameless.

"So bad," I repeated, shaking my head.

The rest of the ceremony was pretty much torture, fingers laced together, waiting for the moment when we could kiss again.

After the final blessing, everyone started leaving the church as we signed the register. Arnauld, the photographer of the fake photo shoot, had been taking pictures of us throughout the ceremony.

He guided us and told us what to do as he took a few more pictures with the help of his "assistants," a mix of

A Scottish Wedding

photographers and wedding planners.

"Okay, now it's time for you two to make your way outside," Fern said as he approached us. "Remember, big smiles! These pictures are going to be everywhere!"

"What's Fern doing here?" Hugh asked, puzzled. "Why is he wearing the same headset as Sandra?"

"That would be because he is our *wedding planner*."

"Fern is our wedding planner? I was jealous of a wedding planner?"

I nodded, adding in a slight eye roll for emphasis.

"That's right. Besides, he is positively gay. Your jealousy was completely unnecessary."

"And you've been organizing this wedding this whole time? Is that why you two always looked up to no good?"

"That's right! And we did it right under your nose, MacLeod!"

He wrapped his arms around my waist.

"Now, I wouldn't get so cocky if I were you, *wife*."

"Oh yeah? Why, what are you going to do about it?"

"You'll just have to wait and see."

Chapter 20

SAM

"Hey, what did Fern mean by 'these pictures are going to be everywhere'?" Hugh asked before we even made it out of the church.

"Well, in order to be able to pull all this off, I had to sell my soul to the devil . . . meaning I had to give Nora something in exchange for the day off and halting production."

"What did you have to trade, Sam?"

"The photo shoot . . . *your* photo shoot . . . it's actually going to be a spread in *Scottish Brides and their Grooms*," I told him, gritting my teeth. I was afraid of his reaction.

He didn't like the media butting in on our relationship, and only used the press to his advantage when we needed to get the network off our back.

A Scottish Wedding

"So, there's no formalwear campaign? That was a cover-up?" he asked.

"Please don't be mad." I clutched my bouquet in my hands a little tighter.

A laugh erupted from his chest, and the smile that stretched across his face made me stupid.

"No, I'm not mad. I'm almost relieved, in a way. I wasn't sure about some of those outfits," he said, running a hand through his hair. We both laughed.

Fern motioned for us to start walking down the nave of the church, and Hugh offered me his arm. We took all of three steps before we stopped again.

"What is it?"

He nodded to my flowers. "Your bouquet. I'm just now noticing it."

One of the few things I'd really wanted was a bouquet made of heather. It was a symbol of our love and such an important part of our relationship. I'd fallen in love with Scotland when he'd shown me the heather in bloom, and later I had fallen in love with him.

The man at my side.

My husband.

Since it was already late September, the heather was pretty scarce on the glen. We had to have the florist find it for us, and he was also able to find something else.

Something *rare*.

"Is that white heather?"

"That's correct. I have to thank your niece for that. She insisted I use regular heather *and* white heather for my bouquet."

"White heather is rare, and it's a symbol of good luck."

"She said the heather turns white if a fairy steps on it."

He smiled, as if remembering something. "My grandma used to tell me the same legend."

Our gazes locked, and he reached for my face with his free hand. He brushed his fingers along my cheek and leaned down to kiss me again.

He paused before his lips touched mine.

"I would very much like to kiss you again, *wife*. May I?" he asked in a gruff tone.

A laugh escaped my lips. "You may kiss me again, *husband*."

I wrapped my arms around his neck as his lips and his tongue conquered and possessed my mouth, sending a jolt of electricity down my spine.

I wasn't aware of much else in that moment. There was my heart beating loudly in my ears, his lips on mine, and the bright beam of Arnauld's flash as the photographer took a candid shot of us.

"So, where are we going next?" Hugh asked. We were in the back seat of the Mercedes as the driver took us to our wedding reception. We had taken so many pictures on the hill behind the church, until the weather changed drastically and thin, icy rain drops had started falling over us.

"Did you ever find a castle?" The tone of amusement in his voice wasn't lost on me. I had told him how hard it was to find anything available, one of the few details I'd shared with him when he'd gotten restless about us not setting a date.

"No," I said in a resigned tone. "I really wanted a castle for the reception, but none of them were very close to the church in Stonehaven, and the ones that were within an hour or two were all booked up. I even signed up for cancelations, but nothing. No one canceled!" I told him in an exasperated tone.

He chuckled. "Wait a moment, are you actually upset no one canceled their wedding?"

"I've done worse," I confessed.

"What could you possibly have done?" He was flat-out laughing at me now.

I pursed my lips together. "I went as far as to offer a trade to the couple who was getting married this weekend. I offered them VIP passes to *Abarath*'s premiere."

"You didn't." His eyes sparkled with glee.

"I did, and they refused. So, I tried to bribe them with something else."

"Something else?"

"Guest-starring roles on the show! I mean, who would pass that up, right? All they had to do was postpone their wedding a measly *twelve months*." I pressed my lips together, trying not to laugh. "I've done ridiculous things to make this wedding happen, Hugh. I just hope you love every bit of it."

"Sam, don't be silly. How could I not love it? You know that only one thing mattered to me, and that has happened already." He lifted my hand, placing a kiss on my ring finger, just above the wedding band he'd slid onto it an hour prior.

I licked my lips, and he noticed.

The intense, dark look in his eyes was too much for me. This time, I initiated the kiss, molding my lips to his.

Unfortunately, our driver soon told us we'd reached our destination.

Since castles were hard to come by—or more accurately, they were booked way too far in advance—Fern and I had ended up having to settle for something different.

He found the most adorable rustic barn available for weddings and private events and with his vision and talent, he turned it into a fairy tale with a multitude of white flowers and twinkling lights.

Instead of having a sit-down dinner and dealing with seating charts, we opted for buffets and open tables. That way, people were able to mingle and socialize as they pleased.

The menu included an equal amount of American and Scottish dishes.

We had cullen skink soup with smoked haddock, potatoes and onions and haggis with neeps and tatties, a dish made with turnips and potatoes. On another table there was prime rib roast served with mashed potatoes, gravy, and green beans, as well as smoked salmon. Fern was thoughtful enough to think we should add a couple of vegetarian dishes; I was particularly fond of the deep-

A Scottish Wedding

fried goat cheese with marinated grilled vegetables and the herb risotto served with a side of pan-fried garlic mushrooms.

A lemon tart with Chantilly cream occupied one side of the dessert table, while little glasses filled with cranachan—a Scottish dessert made from a mixture of whipped cream, whisky, honey, and fresh raspberries—decorated the other side.

In the middle, there was the thing I was most proud of.

The thing I believed Hugh would like the most.

"A s'mores wedding cake?" Hugh asked in a tone that was a mix of surprise and delight. That's right, my handsome Scot had a weakness for the delicious, messy treat he'd discovered when he lived in LA. I had found out for myself during a romantic weekend following our post-Oscars reunion just how much he couldn't say no to the melted chocolate and marshmallow smashed between two crunchy graham crackers.

"You're full of surprises . . . *wife*." He looked at me with a certain wicked glint. He'd used the word a couple of times already, but it was certainly going to take a while before the word lost its charm and effect.

Or maybe that would never happen. Maybe every single time he called me wife, I would feel the same kind of heat pervade my body, and each time, warmth would rise to my cheeks. Maybe each time he called me his wife, I'd feel my heart swell in my chest.

I should be so lucky.

He glanced at the wedding cake again and then his eyes met mine. His smile, stretched and big, illuminated his whole face.

"I still can't believe you did all this. I can't believe we're actually *married*."

I nodded in understanding, as I was experiencing the same feelings of amazement. I couldn't believe we were married. A laugh rose to my lips from deep down in my belly.

"Have I told you lately how much I love you?" he asked me with a big smile that made his eyes shine like precious gems. He was irresistible when he smiled like that.

I smiled, biting the inside of my bottom lip, the light in his eyes igniting a delicious ache in my chest.

"You have the rest of our life to tell me that, *mo gradh*."

What makes a successful wedding?

Is it the amount of alcohol consumed? Can a wedding be declared successful based exclusively on the quality of the food? Or the number of attendees who dance tirelessly through the night? Or simply the fact that the guests didn't seem to get tired of partying? In any case, we were in the running for one of the most successful weddings ever.

The band had been playing for hours, and none of the attendees seemed ready to leave. My dashing husband and I danced to several songs, including Ed Sheeran's "How Would You Feel" and Foy Vance's "Guiding Light." For our first dance, I'd picked Tori Kelly's "I Was Made For Loving You." The lyrics of the song spoke to me and reminded me

A Scottish Wedding

of the way Hugh and I met. Just like in the song, it had all started with a stranger's hand clutched in mine. Or more accurately, with my hand in Hugh's hand.

Who would have known that a hike on an early morning and a casual meeting with a stranger would have changed my life? Hugh's strong arms enveloped me as we slow danced for a while, lost in each other's eyes. His embrace was my favorite place to be, cocooned by his arms and his steady heartbeat.

If God was willing, I was going to fall asleep in my husband's embrace for the rest of my life.

I danced with my father, my father-in-law, and each one of my brothers-in-law. Surprisingly, Tamhas was the one with the best moves of all.

I listened to jokes and stories about Hugh's childhood. I met relatives I hadn't had the chance to see before. I welcomed every toast and shot of whisky until I was just a bit too tipsy and knew I had to stop.

A couple of hours later, I found myself rushing to the restroom—I hadn't gone to the bathroom since I'd put on my wedding dress earlier in the day.

I had never been anyone's bridesmaid before, so I had no idea how complicated it was to go to the bathroom on your own. I tried . . . and I got stuck trying to lift my dress and pee at the same time. I chuckled to myself in the empty bathroom, thinking it wasn't fair that my husband's outfit had such easier access.

In the end, I had to come out of the restroom, my bladder about to burst, and looked for either my mother or one of my bridesmaids.

"My feet are killing me," my sister huffed, exasperated

as she held my dress up while I was peeing.

"Mine aren't."

"Don't rub it in," she mused.

"Sorry, I should have thought of getting flats for my bridesmaids, too."

"Nahhh, don't worry about it, but I should obviously follow your lead more often."

"Obviously."

Amira made sure I was good to go before leaving me alone in the restroom. She seemed to be in a hurry to go back, and I wondered if it was about Melissa or not. In all the madness of planning the wedding, I hadn't had a chance to ask her what was going on between the two of them. I knew they were on *friendly* terms, but I had no clue if they wanted to take their relationship to the next level. After all, they lived so far away from each other, and long-distance relationships were never easy.

I told Amira to go ahead and leave, and took my time washing my hands and fixing my hair and makeup. Cecilia had done such a great job with it; she'd wanted to return the favor after I did the makeup on the day of her wedding.

I fixed the slightly smudged eyeliner in the corners and stared at my eyes, which looked bigger and wider with the help of fake lashes. She'd used earthy tones for my eye shadow and eyeliner, and had shaped my eyebrows to make my arches look even longer.

She'd applied a long-lasting deep mauve lipstick that was miraculously still in place even after all the times I'd kissed Hugh.

The foundation and the powder she'd used were still

holding up thanks to the finishing spray. I fixed the low bun at the nape of my neck and the flowers the hairstylist had inserted in the knot then marched out of the bathroom, ready to dance for the rest of the night.

But, when I stepped out, I was surprised to see everyone turn in my direction, giving me big smiles, just as they had when I walked down the nave of the church earlier in the morning.

What's going on? Why is everyone looking at me? And where is Hugh?

I noticed the band wasn't playing anymore, and I wondered if they had taken a break. I walked around, waving at the guests, but I noticed everyone was sort of frozen on the spot, not chatting, not eating, not having any kind of fun.

The lights went down a bit, making it just a little harder to see.

Where was my family? Where was Amira, Rob, Cecilia?

Just then, the band started playing again.

I recognized the notes of the song right away, and a smile stretched across my face immediately.

Everlong.

He'd remembered. He'd remembered the conversation I'd had with Cecilia weeks ago about my favorite love song.

I was smiling like a fool, and I couldn't wait to see his face.

That rascal.

I decided to walk closer to the stage where the band was playing and I finally spotted Amira and Melissa's silhouettes as well as my brother, my parents and their spouses, and my in-laws.

But . . . where was *he*?

Then, the singer of the band sang the first verse of the song.

My eyes shot up, I looked over to the stage, and my gaze met the most incredible view.

No, Hugh hadn't gotten the Foo Fighters to come play at our wedding, but somehow he'd convinced all his brothers to play the song with him.

For me.

My eyes had never seen anything quite like it.

Five Scottish brothers, dressed to the nines in their best kilts, playing one of the best songs ever written. They looked wickedly handsome, and they didn't sound that bad, either. I hadn't even known they could play instruments.

My mouth was ajar, face still stunned with wonder.

I had to be dreaming. I almost wanted to pinch myself, but someone else took care of that as she came up to my side. Cecilia pinched my arm slightly and said something I didn't quite grasp.

I felt like I was in a daze.

This was the second time Hugh had done this to me.

And this time he was playing a *guitar*! He'd never even told me he could play!

Cecilia guided me through the small crowd as I wordlessly took in the whole scene.

Hugh, Declan, and Fergus were on guitars and sang the lyrics together, Tamhas was on bass, and the rambunctious Ewan was on drums, doing his best Taylor Hawkins impression.

The scene was bound to cause ladyboners left and

A Scottish Wedding

right.

You can have the other four, ladies. That one is all mine.

Phones were held up high in the air, trying to capture the absolutely scrumptious performance the MacLeod brothers were putting on.

Heart in my throat, I locked eyes with my husband as the thumping of my heart echoed Ewan's beat on the drums. I was on the verge of tears, but thankfully I managed to blink them away. When Hugh gave one of those delicious grins of his, I couldn't help but smile back, and I started singing the song along with him at the top of my lungs.

I pulled the bobby pins out of my hair and dropped them on the floor, throwing away the flowers pinned in my hair, letting my waves spill over my shoulders. I started jumping on the spot, as if I were attending the most exclusive rock concert.

Just like the song said, I wondered if things would always be this good between us, but I knew all too well that life and marriage were not like in the movies, not like a love song. It was all the good and fluffy feelings, but also hard work and sometimes heartbreak.

As I sang the song out loud with my husband and everyone else around me, I hoped we could always remember how much we loved each other and the promises we'd made one to another.

When the song was over, it was a mayhem of cheers.

No one cheered as loud as drunk Scots having fun.

I barely gave him time to put the guitar down and step off the stage before I threw myself at him, almost knocking the breath out of him.

He laughed in my ear as he held my chest close to him. He swung me around as if we were dancing and I covered his face with kisses, ignoring the thin layer of sweat on his jaw and his neck. I was acting like an infatuated groupie, but I was past the point of caring.

I needed my fill of him. He was looking entirely too delectable for me to be indifferent to his charms. He put me down on the floor just as the band started playing Neil Young's "Harvest Moon" and I wrapped my arms around his neck, swaying with him.

"Is this how it's going to be?" I asked, and he replied with an amused frown.

"What do you mean?"

"Are we going to keep surprising each other at every possible occasion?"

"God, I hope so," he replied with a devilish smile. "I don't think I've recovered from the shock of seeing you walk down the aisle yet."

"And I don't think I will ever recover from seeing you play my favorite love song."

"I hope we didn't sound too rough. We've only been practicing for a few weeks."

"How could you even . . . ?"

"I did it when you weren't in my trailer. As it turns out, the network's rules of conduct for us kind of played in my favor. My brothers and I rehearsed over video chat. It wasn't easy, and I thought we had a few more months to rehearse. Now that I think about it, it makes perfect sense!"

"What does?"

"The fact that Declan was so hard on me and kept telling me to rehearse any free moment I had. *He knew!*"

"He did," I confessed. "Pretty much everyone here was in on it. I couldn't have done it without them."

"You did great."

He held my gaze, eyes clouded with love, lust, and a bit of drunkenness. He leaned down, his lips less than an inch away from mine. His hands fell lower on my hips, and then he gave my *arse* a squeeze.

"Now, a soft kiss. Aye, by that kiss, I vow an endless bliss." He said the words solemnly, placing his lips on mine in a chaste kiss that paved the way for a more tumultuous, intense, spellbinding, breathtaking one. He kissed my mouth and possessed my tongue until I was dizzy. I thought about the quote and frowned, trying to guess whose it was.

"Lord Byron?" I asked.

"John Keats," he whispered in my ear. He pulled back, studying my features a little more, and I fell prey to his hypnotic gaze. My eyes fell on his lips, and impulse took over. I needed more. I needed another blissful kiss. I leaned forward to kiss him, but he pulled back.

"You're such a damn tease!" I said, scrunching up my nose. "I am your *wife*! Kiss me or else!" I pulled away from his embrace, but he wouldn't let go.

Instead, he burst out laughing and held me even tighter. I was flush against his chest and I could feel it shaking with laughter. I couldn't help it—I ended up laughing with him.

Our families and friends, momentarily distracted by our playful bickering, smiled and looked lovingly upon us.

"That's right. You are my *wife*, my Sam." His eyes

softened, and he gave me a look full of adoration. He kissed my forehead first, the tip of my nose next, and my lips last. He lingered on them, alternating soft kisses with more urgent ones that did nothing but undermine my self-control. I almost forgot about everyone else around us.

"Let's go home, Hugh MacLeod. You look like you're drunk," I whispered playfully in his ear.

"Drunk on whisky? Maybe. Drunk on you? *Definitely*."

Thank you for reading!

Acknowledgements

First off, I need to thank the readers! Thank you for loving Lost in Scotland! Without your feedback, support and encouragement, there wouldn't be a sequel!

I hope you love A Scottish Wedding as much as I do.

Thanks to my wonderful editor, Caitlin with Editing by C. Marie. It's always a pleasure working with you. You give me peace of mind and make my words better, and that's invaluable.

Thanks to Marla Esposito with Proofing Style, for her outstanding work.

Thanks to Emily, for loving this story when it was just a bunch of scenes all over the place. Thanks to Mae Wood and Zeia Jameson, for being on this journey with me.

Samantha with Samantha Leigh Design: thank you for another wonderful cover! A Scottish Wedding looks so beautiful next to Lost in Scotland.

Thanks to Alexandria with AB Formatting: I can always count on you!

Thanks to Enticing Journey, The Elite Reader and Love Kissed Book Promotion, Itsy Bitsy Book Bits for handling the promo.

My wonderful readers group, Hilaria Alexander Rockettes! I love your sass, ladies. Thank you for listening to my ramblings and loving my words.

Lauren Brynolf, I hope this is the beginning of a beautiful friendship. Thank you for agreeing to help me out.

A big, huge thank you to all the wonderful women of the indie community who inspire me on a daily basis and make me want to become a better version of myself. There are too many of you to name, but you know who you are.

Manuscript Minxes, thank you for the daily motivation! I love the way we keep supporting each other!

Thanks to the bloggers who rock my socks off and work tirelessly to promote the work of indie authors. I couldn't do this without your help.

A special thank you to Abeautifulbookblog, Prisoners of Print, Schmexy Girl Book Blog, Maryse Book Blog, Typical Distractions, Aaly and The Books, Reviews by Reds, Disheveled Book Blog, Reading in Sarah's Corner, A Page to Turn Reviews, ItaPixie's Book Corner, Marieke's Books, Beauty and her Books. Thank you for supporting me.

Playlist

This is just a small selection of the music I listened to while writing A Scottish Wedding. You can play the entire playlist on Spotify!

How Would You Feel – Ed Sheeran
You Da One – Rihanna
Fake Love – Drake
Third of May – Fleet Foxes
Cranes in the Sky – Solange
Redbone – Childish Gambino
Hello – Erykah Badu
All I Want is You – U2
I Was Made For Loving You – Tori Kelly ft. Ed Sheeran
Guidin Light – Foy Vance ft. Ed Sheeran
Let's Stay Together – Al Green
Everlong – Foo Fighters

About the Author

Hilaria Alexander was born and raised in the south of Italy, where her family still lives. She was bit by the travel bug early on and lived in Tokyo and Orlando for a while before settling down in Oklahoma City with her husband and kids.

She loves books—obviously—as well as movies and TV, and is addicted to award shows. She can't play an instrument to save her life, but she loves music, which is one of her biggest inspirations when plotting new stories.

If you have questions about her or her books, ask her on Facebook and Twitter, or email her at hilaria_alexander@outlook.com.

For excerpts, news and giveaways, join her readers group, Hilaria Alexander Rockettes.

ALSO AVAILABLE BY HILARIA ALEXANDER

Prude

My editor, who also happens to be my best friend, told me she thinks I write like a prude. That EVERYONE thinks I write like a prude. She made it clear that my next book will not be published if I don't "spice things up".

Instead of replying calmly, like the "old" Prudence Clearwater would have, I stormed out of her office and told her to go to hell.

After a few days spent wallowing, unsure about my future, I decided that I should:

1. Ignore the naysayers and backstabbing.
2. Re-evaluate my inner circle, especially my deceitful BFF.
3. Focus on my writing and figure out where I went wrong.
4. Accept any help I can get, especially from my old college crush, who happens to be a successful book agent and looks like a Viking God.
5. Keep my friendship with the aforementioned Viking God platonic, even when he makes me tingle in all the right places.

Or maybe, since I'm not a prude, I should just live a little...and surrender to the charming Ben Hallstrom.

What's the worst that could happen?

Music brought them together,
But it just might tear them apart.

Leaving New York.
It was the best decision I ever made.
Packing up and moving to the other side of the world changed me.
I turned a new page, leaving the past behind.

Amsterdam felt like home–for a while.
But I was still stuck.
Unable to move forward.

Then, Lou Rivers showed up,
Instantly, I felt my life shift again.
A constant reminder of the life I once had,
The mistakes I left behind.
He's the musician I dreamed of being...
If I were stronger, bolder, braver.
But I wasn't.

He taught me how to love music again,
And for the first time, I feel like I know what to do.
But how can I?
How can I become myself without giving up on us?

FU Cancer

Lucy has always been a good girl. The most hardcore thing she's done in her life was falling for a divorced man ten years her senior.

But he was the love of her life, and she married him. When her Peter Pan of a husband decided to divorce her, she thought it was her chance to start anew. That was until she was diagnosed with breast cancer. Besides looking like Britney circa 2007, she is taking it well, real well. You might see her walk around the hospital during chemo sessions with bright colored wigs and outrageous t-shirts that seem to shock the most conservative employees. One of them reads FU CANCER.

Not About Love

Strong and independent,
Wrong for each other in every way.
But the heat, the passion, the pull.
Undeniable.
Irresistible.
When we were together,
The chaos turned to desire,
Need.
Bliss.
I was his.
He was mine.
For the time-being.
Different countries.
Different worlds.
Just sex.
No strings attached.
That's how Boyd Rivers wanted it.
And exactly how I liked it.
But sometimes, fate has other plans...
Can it really be not about love?